# Sons of Granada

# SONS

*of*

# GRANADA

A Novel

## CARL JERONIMO

*Albaicin Press*
*New York, 2016*

"Carve, friends, from stone and dream,
in the Alhambra, a barrow for the poet,
on the water of fountains that weep
and whisper, for eternity:
'the crime was in Granada,
in his Granada!'"

—ANTONIO MACHADO

*A gentleman commenting to his wife while walking on a
street in Granada, seeing a beggar with outstretched hand*

"Dale limosna, mujer,
que no hay en la vida nada
como la pena de ser
ciego en Granada."

"Give him alms, woman,
there is nothing worse
than being blind
in Granada"

—FRANCISCO A. DE ICAZA

**FEDERICO GARCÍA LORCA**

History accounts that Federico Garcia Lorca, the beloved Spanish poet and playwright, internationally acclaimed and adored, was executed in Andalucia in the first days of the brutal Spanish Civil War. The whereabouts of his remains, as well as those of thousands of Spanish patriots, are unknown to this day.

# CHAPTER 1

"FEDERICO! FEDERICO! Where are you?" The little boy sat in the rain as cold sheets of water cascaded on his face. He looked up at the sky where two black birds were crossing the field. The gray clouds were angry, the boy thought, and they wanted to swallow the little birds. *Poor birds*, thought Federico, as rivulets of warm tears flowed down his cheeks. He stared at the ground in front of him and noticed the lifeless body of a black bird in a shallow puddle as water continued to stream down his round face from his jet-black hair. He looked all around him as the wind and rain swept the *vega*, the fertile plain and open fields where his father planted their crops. "Federico! Federico!" He stood up so that his mother Vincenta could see him. The frantic woman held her hand on her brow surveying the countryside, spotted the boy, and ran toward him. The rain continued to relentlessly pour down and flashes of lightning streaked through the sky.

"What are you doing?" His anxious mother scolded. "Is that bird dead, mama? Did he do something wrong?" His small hand wiped the mixture of tears and raindrops from his furrowed brow.

"No, Federico, he did nothing wrong," Vincenta replied. Perhaps he was sick, the child rationalized. "Come, let us go back to the house and change your clothes. Why do you sit in the rain alone? Come! Come! Quickly, now!" Federico took one last glance at the dead creature as the puddle became deeper and started to envelop its entire body. The lifeless dark form frightened him, for he did not understand death. The sky and the earth must talk to each other, he thought.

As his mother grasped his hand to lead him back to the house, the rain began to descend from the skies with even more vigor. Just then, a swarm of black birds above squawked, and the little boy looked upward to watch them fly to safety. He was glad the heavens had not spit them out as they had the birds' brother.

# CHAPTER 2

C ARLOS SMILED as he walked down *Cuesta de los Chinos* at six
o'clock in the morning, reflecting that it was his favorite thing
to do in Granada. The cobblestone path winding down the rear
side of the Alhambra, the red fortress, had been a favorite walkway for
hundreds of years and at this moment, it was all his. It was completely
quiet except for the sound of water rushing from the mountain above,
which the Moors expertly channeled through stone trenches or *ace-
quias* to their baths and the gardens surrounding their palace. The great
red walls loomed above him to his left as he wended his way down the
steep descent from the fortress. Olive trees lined the narrow walkway
on both sides and sloping banks of lush greenery and colorful bougainvillea rose up on his right. A few small, whitewashed houses with red-
tiled roofs lined the path on his right and appeared to be of comparatively modest construction — stuck, as if by caste system, beneath the
grandeur towering above. Ghosts of Moorish sentinels looked down
from atop the Alhambra's vermilion walls — a constant reminder that
this magnificence was theirs and never to be relinquished. He had
walked this route hundreds of times, for the Alhambra pulled him in
at its will. He returned often to this sacred place to visit family, the

*chirimoya* farmers who lived close by in Almuñecar. Carlos thought of himself as having been transported back in time—an eerie feeling that connected him to the ancients who strolled here in a prior era. He also reflected on how difficult it was to describe this awesome and entrancing power of the Alhambra to someone who had not visited this majestic site. The stories of the Alhambra and its many intrigues were one reason he was here.

But Carlos' reason for this visit owed itself to a different purpose. It stemmed from the tale of one favorite son of the Alhambra and Granada—a poet—and was Carlos' true motivation for this trip. He was determined to research the mystery that had perplexed the world and fascinated the Spanish nation for some time: the puzzling circumstances surrounding the death of one of Spain's most famous contemporary poets. Many of the Spaniards he talked to offered few details about the murder on that August night more than forty years ago in 1936. Few cared to engage him on the subject. Here in Granada it has never been a welcomed subject. The people tired long ago of the constant rehashing of those terrible days of war and destruction, and have preferred to forget the atrocities committed by both sides in that war that divided the region's families.

The dead poet's works and life intrigued Carlos since he was first introduced to the dazzling poetry of this young, handsome man while studying Spanish literature in University. Though dead for so long, his presence was alive and still very much felt here in Granada.

Carlos had begun his career writing travelogues and stories about Spain for an assortment of American magazines. He felt a special attachment to this country he considered his adopted homeland. But he was tiring of earning a living this way, realizing that it did not fulfill his expectations. His interests were changing and his writing was taking a different course.

He thought much more about writing something of meaning—something of significance. The dead poet, Federico García Lorca, held Carlos' deep interest and rendered a compelling story that needed to be unraveled. Perhaps, he thought, he could delve more deeply into that mystery. The circumstances surrounding Lorca's death might provide the perfect setting for a novel he had been contemplating. Carlos thought of himself as an adept writer and the possibility of conquering a new genre intrigued him.

He had reviewed many times the sequence of events leading up to the poet's death by reading newspaper accounts, biographies, and histories written from a variety of different perspectives. Most of these left muddled and unclear the events of that day. An unfortunate legacy of the terrible conflict people wanted to forget left many of the unspeakable happenings that occurred during that period without closure. It seemed to Carlos that people just preferred this kind of amnesia. But slowly, Carlos was piecing together what he thought might be a feasible account of those days.

The understanding at that time among most Spaniards held that rebel soldiers of the Spanish Civil War of 1936 had murdered Lorca, the rising young poet and playwright.

Why he had been executed in the very first days of the Civil War during that hot August was a burdensome weight Spain has neither been able to shed nor fully comprehend.

The more discoveries Carlos made in his research, the more he was convinced this was a fascinating tale that needed to be retold to those who had never heard of the young author who met violent death so tragically and abruptly.

Federico García Lorca had many times walked the identical route Carlos now trod and must have likewise been in awe of this same hauntingly beautiful landscape Carlos was eagerly taking in. In this and other ways, Carlos felt a curious alliance with the martyred poet. It was more an intuitive or visceral impulse than anything else—leaving Carlos connected to Lorca for reasons he found difficult to rationalize or understand. Some voice inside pulled him toward the poet, a writer like himself. He also found shallow and without merit the standard explanations of Lorca's sudden and unanticipated execution. Carlos repeatedly combed through the scores of photographs of the poet he'd uncovered in the many books he devoured on the subject. The image of the round-faced Lorca with his unmistakable smile now continuously danced before him. He was determined to revisit that brutal period and study the details of Lorca's last earthly days once again.

Carlos surveyed his surroundings, recounting the events that occurred on that hot and humid morning in August, 1936 as he circled down and around the Alhambra—traversing the Rio Darro atop a narrow ancient stone bridge, el Puente Cabrera. Built by the Romans, the structure enters into the *Albayzin,* the oldest barrio of this ancient city, by way of the *Paseo de los Tristes,* the Walk of Sadness. The horrifying events that would forever change Lorca's life now thoroughly enveloped Carlos in their siren call.

He looked up, taking note of the majestic mountains that bordered the city. Granada was extraordinarily beautiful—surrounded on the one side by the snow-capped Sierra Nevadas, and the lush fertile *vega*s—the gentle plains that lie at their feet. From his vantage point near the Alhambra, looking toward the southeast, were vast rolling valleys where farms, bridges and small villages were scattered as far as the eye could see. To the northeast, steep hills shot off in the direction of Jaen, another important Moorish city.

Granada exists within the confluence of three great rivers that contain so much Spanish history, the Beiro, Genil and Darro. It was the perfect setting for past civilizations that flourished there.

Carlos enjoyed the warm breeze that lightly brushed his face. Granada's climate varies by season—like this summer day, hot and humid. The heat bearing down from cloudless skies was unrelentingly oppressive, with steam rising from the scalding pavement. Refuge was often sought in the hundreds of small cafés that exist everywhere throughout this city of narrow streets and alleyways. They would serve cold beer, chilled wine, and ice cold water, and offer several minutes of relief from the uncompromising sun.

By contrast, the region was cold and damp in the winter, with occasional snowfall and freezing temperatures. All types of vegetation thrived in the *vegas*; fruit trees of all varieties gave it an Eden-like appearance. Palm and date trees, avocado and orange, lemon and pear and scores of other fruit and nut trees abounded—even in the private gardens of Granada's city dwellers. Exotic fruits from the *nispero, loquat,* and *caqui* trees were favorites in the local markets.

The grandest of all of southern Spain's trees is the olive tree, which is visible as far as the eye can see. Neat rows mark the landscape from Granada to Cordoba, the ancient Moorish capital to the west, and toward Jaen, the city to the north. These trees that bear fruit and oil, Andalucia's liquid gold, are the lifeline of the region. *Aceitunas*—olives—are included in every small or large meal and are served in hundreds of different ways.

Amidst all this abundance are sweet smelling flowers: jasmine, rose, orange blossom, bougainvillea, iris, and the wallflowers that decorate every corner of the shops and homes of the city.

The pomegranate is Granada's most sacred fruit and from whence comes its Arabic name, *Gárnata.* It has a symbolic tie to the city dating back to the time of the Moors. In the Qur'an, the holy scripture of the Moors, pomegranates grew in paradise. To Carlos, Granada was *his* paradise—that evidence widely on display throughout the city. Stylistic representations of this fruit appear on street markers, mosaic designs and sculptures that adorn building entrances and sidewalks—its motif woven intrinsically into the fabric of daily life.

Carlos gazed at the terraced mountains thinking that none of these lands had been exploited now as they were by the Moors, Granada's proud ancestors. They were consummate stewards of their environment and agriculture. Among their famous accomplishments are the gardens of the Alhambra called *Generalife* in Spanish and *Janat al-Arif,* or "Architect's Garden" in Arabic. They are the jewels that adorn the Alhambra, and are a living testament to the Moors' genius and engineering prowess. These gardens, where Carlos passed many hours, are still cultivated today and had once supplied the inhabitants of the terra cotta-hued fortress, which at one time numbered forty thousand, with food and flowers. The landscaped gardens have been masterfully integrated into the mountainside design next to the Alhambra and mesh artfully with the architectural theme of the Moors. They were nourished by the perpetual downward flow of water from the mountain streams above, which the Moors skillfully harnessed.

Thousands of tourists have made their way here to visit this ancient mountaintop fortress and its gardens that exist in such perfect harmony with Granada.

From this perch, the Alhambra has for centuries kept a maternalistic eye on all that has transpired in its city below, Carlos reflected—the mother of Granada. The long walls that emanate from the Alhambra, once useful in keeping out its enemies, cling to the mountainsides surrounding the inhabitants of this city like the arms of a mother protecting her children.

Granada's history fascinated Carlos. It is an ancient city. Its roots are Celtic, Phoenician, Carthaginian, Greek, Byzantine, Ibero-Visigoth, and finally, or almost finally, Arab—whom the Spaniards call Moors. They were travelers who arrived from Africa by way of Damascus, in present-day Syria, during the eighth century.

These Moors, conquerors and inhabitants of this region, known to them as Al-Andaluz and today as Andalucia, or "land of the Vandals," developed one of the the first civilized and progressive cultures known to Europe. Al-Andaluz, the very antithesis of its name, was the center of European culture and learning at a time when the countries that surrounded it—France, England, and Germany—were comparatively primitive and barely awakening. Scholars have said that while the Moors studied the philosophies and sciences of the Greeks, Charlemagne was learning how to write his name.

*Granadino* architecture, agriculture, libraries of letters, philosophy and governmental organization were among the most advanced and esteemed in the known world for several centuries. The Andalusian philosophers and intellectuals from the capital city of Cordoba, the Moorish Mecca of the West, were renown throughout the civilized world. They brought to Europe the Greek philosophers Plato and Socrates, and mathematicians Euclid, Pythagoras, and Archimedes. They translated their works initially to Arabic, then to Latin and finally to the vulgar Romance languages of Spanish and Gallic.

Most present day *Granadino*s abandon their city in the summer for the surrounding beaches of Salobreña, Almuñecar, Almería and Malaga—all which were once part of the greater kingdom of Granada and founded by the Moors. Carlos visited often, and enjoyed fresh fish, octopus, and shellfish in addition to the cool ocean breezes that offered respite from the tortuous heat of the interior cities.

Notwithstanding this, Carlos reasoned, the streets would be barren in any case at this hour of the morning, for Granada, like most Spanish cities, is nocturnal. He understood the Spanish culture, where most activities begin late in the evening and last through the early morning hours. He looked forward to spending his evenings in the Gypsy caves of the El Albayzin, preferring the *Granadino* nights to its hot summer days—remaining in the caves usually until the first rays of dawn, when the hauntingly melodic Gypsy music would finally come to an end.

Carlos recognized that the soul of Granada was its music. The sounds that filled the night air were the pride of the city. The *Cante Jondo,* or deep song, is the most traditional and native sound. It's given voice and meaning to this city. Purely Andalusian in origin, it is derived from an intermingling of ancient Byzantine Christian liturgies, Saracen Moorish influences and the strong Gypsy presence in the region following its arrival in Spain from northern Africa in the early part of the fifteenth century. At that time, Spain was comprised of *taifas,* or small independent kingdoms divided between the Christians and Moors.

These sad ballads, life stories recounted in deep, throaty verse, and emanating directly from the soul, are accompanied by clapping . . . shouts of despair . . . *Ay! Ay!* . . . and then long moments of silence.

They are a reflection of humanity's struggle, life and death — the constant grind and alienation felt by the common people. Carlos thought they exuded sadness and believed their echoes hung like a cloud over the city — a sadness he knew derived from Granada's tumultuous history. The ballads were sung by women both slim and stout, young handsome men, old toothless grandfathers, and young children. It was their bread of daily life. The pain and tragic history of this music became Carlos' guide to the city. He often thought to himself that if he stayed long enough and listened carefully, he could recognize and absorb its power. Carlos intuited he could hear it in the trees . . . in the city's streets and buildings, and in the rushing waters of its rivers Darro, Genil and Beiro. He heard it in the caves of the nearby Albayzin, inhabited for centuries by Gypsies that clustered the hills beside the Darro River, with the Alhambra looming above.

The guitar became this music's grand companion and dance transformed it into the vibrant, fast-moving *Flamenco* of today. Its strong emotion overwhelmed yet invigorated Carlos. It was exhilarating listening to the rapidly strumming guitars accompanied by deep, raspy voices, and drinking wine until the morning light of a new day signaled the evening's end.

The fate of one person, the handsome young poet, playwright, musician, and *Granadino*, was also entranced by these sounds of his city. Despite living during one of Spain's darkest periods, his intriguing existence was solely responsible for Carlos' presence there at that time. For Carlos, it was an easy decision to set aside an entire summer in pursuit of the author's fate, as he was steadfast in his belief that Lorca's short life was perhaps the most tragic and dramatic of all of Granada's stories.

Carlos wanted to understand the brutality of the Spanish Civil War. He wondered what caused a man to fight against and even hate his own brother and neighbor. But of far greater interest to Carlos was why the lore of Lorca's death had survived in everyone's mind for so long, more than forty years, when so many others had met the same fate as he. And even more perplexing was why anyone would kill a poet? What had Lorca done to sustain so drastic a fate?

Carlos pondered who still might still be alive to remember the poet's last days after so many years. Certainly there were many in Granada. Would anyone dare speak with him on a topic that had been taboo to discuss under the forty-year dictatorship of General Francisco Franco? The war was still fresh in the minds of many and too difficult to recount even now. Carlos suspected the answers to his questions were both complicated and hidden from plain sight. This would become his quest—to discover exactly why and how Lorca had perished. This was the missing and critical ingredient for a new recounting of a tale he would bring back into the public's consciousness.

Carlos proceeded toward the *Biblioteca Universitaria,* Granada's University library in the old downtown section of Granada. It was a good place to begin, where abundant sources of information were certain to be found. Carlos knew it would take time to delve into the history—to form a better picture of what Spain must have been like during those terrible days. But he also knew that to better comprehend those times he would come up against multiple sets of opinions about what actually occurred.

There were those that wanted only to bury the past. They probably would not be helpful as Carlos was seeing by the few inquiries he had already attempted. Then there were those that wanted all the atrocities of that ugly period brought to the light of day. Those were the people he needed to find. They were probably the ones who were most likely to help him. His task would be to assess these opposing lines of thought to form his own conclusions.

Walking down the narrow streets was for him like walking back in time. This pleased Carlos, for he was in Granada and could sense the answers to his questions languishing in the thick, sweltering summer air.

# CHAPTER 3

F RANCI HEREDIA was nervous. He crushed the empty pack of cigarettes in his hand and tossed it into the street. From his coat pocket he took out a fresh pack, fumbled with it as he lit yet another cigarette, and took a deep drag that filled his lungs. As he released a blue cloud of smoke into the hot summer air, his thin, dark body perspired as it always did when he was doing something he didn't like. He ran his fingers through his hair and mopped his forehead. His loose cotton suit hugged his slender features and beneath his jacket, a brightly colored t-shirt revealed wet blotches on his chest.

What did the inspector want this time? He kicked himself thinking of what he had gotten himself into. From the very beginning, he should have taken his punishment, because it could not possibly be worse than this. Every time Inspector De Los Rios wanted to know about something that was taking place in the Gypsy quarter of the Albayzin, it was Franci he turned to. And each time he would have to poke around by listening to the idle talk in the bars, around the caves, and between the street vendors. Information among the Gypsies was a rare commodity, as they were close-mouthed and hardly shared their dealings with even their closest associates. Franci knew he was in for a

long ordeal, but he would have to find out something that would satisfy the inspector. Hopeful as always—if not sooner, then later—he
would usually get a whiff of the sought-after news. He would then be
obliged to relay it to De Los Rios, who would listen and determine if it
satisfied his need. Franci *despised* it. He was disgusted with himself for
informing and reviled the inspector for asking and depending on him.
He knew his freedom had ended when the police caught him trying
to sell some *kif*, the pollen that everyone in Granada smoked, mixing
it with tobacco in their cigarettes. He had committed the grave error
of offering it to a policeman out of uniform. A couple of weeks in jail
would have been preferable to always being within reach of the inspector who never seemed to tire of asking him favors. If any of his friends
even suspected that he passed information to the police from time to
time . . . he shuddered to even think about what the Gypsies might do
to him if they caught wind of his dealings.

He arrived at Plaza Campos 3, the police headquarters in Granada,
and tried to pass unseen up the first flight of stairs to the inspector's
office in the newly remodeled station. Several officers noticed him and
smiled with looks of acknowledgment revealing they were aware he
was being summoned again by De Los Rios. Franci was a Gypsy and
was not supposed to be on this side of the fence. After all, there was
not a single police officer in all of Granada who was a Gypsy! Gypsies and police were like dogs and cats—eternal enemies. The Gypsy's
reputation was that of a thief. In fact, many Gypsies were involved in
the underworld of Granada; but that solely involved the Gypsy underworld. They had never assimilated into the main of Andalusian life, yet
here he was, not remembering how many times he had been here before. It was too late to do anything except maybe leave Granada. But,
the streets were Franci's home and he knew nothing else. The Gypsies
lived in a world completely apart from the normal life and hustle of
Granada. Although they were shopkeepers, innkeepers, and businessmen, living and working in the Albayzin and in *Sacromonte*, they also

conducted other illegal business strictly among themselves. This was the Gypsy tradition that had thrived throughout all of Andalucia.

Although persecuted along with the Moors and Jews who were driven out of Spain by Isabella and Fernando, they had woven themselves into the daily life of Andalucia and especially Granada. Thousands of Gypsies still resided in Spain—their enterprising nightclubs and caves of *Flamenco* attracting most of the tourists who had come to Granada, and which were their constant source of legal revenue. However, distrust of the Gypsies was palpable and as such, they persisted as a source of ridicule. Jokes about Gypsies were commonplace and disrespect for them, rampant. It was impossible to find a *Granadino* who had anything good to say about them, and they were seen as the source of most of the criminal trouble the city had to contend with.

Inspector De Los Rios sat behind his desk, which contained stacks of files and several ashtrays as Franci entered into his corner office. He was an older man with gray hair combed straight back. He removed his glasses as Franci entered this glorified boiler room reeking of smoke. Sitting imposingly on one side, an old wooden filing cabinet was decorated with pictures of the *Alcalde,* the Mayor of Granada, and various citations the inspector had received. Franci thought the inspector must have been at least sixty-five or seventy years of age and wondered why he still did this type of work. The window was open and the hot, sticky breeze from the street below poured into the office, making Franci feel as if he were suffocating. He took a wet handkerchief from his pocket to wipe his face as the inspector greeted him.

*"Hola Franci, me alegro verte"* (It's nice to see you), he said without looking up from his desk. He was short and stocky and gruff in appearance, but with a light in his eyes that pierced people's thoughts—as if allowing him to enter into their minds. This uncanny ability and his many years as a policeman had moved him steadily up the ladder of promotion—his assignments now involving special projects and investigations. Franci sat uneasily as he waited for the inspector to say

something. Inspector De Los Rios understood police work; it was monotonous, time consuming and boring. Repetition was what every good policeman specialized in, and De Los Rios was expert in going over the obvious again and again and again until it led him in a direction that sooner or later would yield results. Finally, he looked up and spoke.

"How are things?" Franci shrugged his shoulders.

"Same as always." The inspector smiled—a smile that Franci knew meant that he was about to ask him another 'favor.'

"What brings me here today, señor, if not for you to inquire of my health? I have a lot to do, and I'm certain you have more to do than be here with me, but there is some talk in the streets that is disturbing."

Franci looked puzzled. "Talk?"

"The Gypsies are up to something; I can't put my finger on just quite what. But I am sure I will know soon … *with a little help*."

It was bad enough that Franci had cooperated with the hated police, but now to have to report on his own people? De Los Rios glared at Franci as would a drill sergent at a new recruit. As the smile disappeared from his face he started shuffling the papers on his desk … "Please close the door behind you."

There was no need to say any more. Franci stood up and began walking toward the door.

"Oh Franci, I am certain that I will be hearing from you very soon … I hope … yes, Franci?"

Franci mumbled incoherently and descended the stairs out of the station and into the streets and the hot noonday sun—hoping to avoid the stares of the people milling around the building.

Carlos selected *A Brief History of Twentieth Century Spain* from the first row of history books he encountered near the front of the library's entrance. Its author was a well-known Socialist in the current government. He leafed through the chapter headings until he came to a section that caught his eye. History was neither his favorite subject nor his favorite approach to understanding how events of the past really occurred. Facts always seemed to be skewed toward the outlook of the writer, who toyed with events according to his particular political bent. The government had done its best for so long to keep that portion of Spain's civil war history covered up and out of public view. Carlos, mindful of this reality, was instead seeking something written between the lines. He was certain he would need to depend more on his own personal conversations and findings. He sorely needed to make contact with those people who actually lived to witness those first gruesome weeks in the capital when soldiers of the insurrection summarily executed scores of people on a daily basis. These individuals neither received fair trials, nor were they permitted any contact with their families. They were simply carted away and executed. Carlos would have to filter through the almost literal mountains of accepted history and rely on his own intuition and investigative acumen.

His anticipated novel would allow him a certain degree of license regarding the poet, as with any historical novel. But the history also had to run parallel to genuine events and demanded accuracy if it were to be acceptable to any publisher. Carlos understood he could not rewrite history, but he could surely bend it to his liking as others had done before him. He glanced around the crowded reading room and spotted a half-empty table. He chose a seat at a corner table near a window and tried to make himself comfortable even as the intense heat flowing into the reading room through the library's open windows was hardly bearable. But after scanning several paragraphs of his selected book, Carlos managed to put the discomfort from the oppressive heat out of his mind and became absorbed in the story of Spain's recent past.

As he read, Carlos began to gain an even greater understanding of the root causes of the antagonisms that overtook the Iberian Peninsula during the 1930s.

War clouds had been brewing on the horizon for years. It came as little surprise when the horrible civil war of 1936 began. In Spain the king and the rich oligarchy had ruled over this country for centuries. Since the reign of the Catholic Monarchs Isabel and Ferdinand in the fifteenth century, power had been consolidated in Madrid, the capital, which maintained sovereignty over all the unruly semi-autonomous regions.

The majority of Spain's population was impoverished rural people who spoke different languages, ate different foods and had different customs and climates. A new young king, Alfonso XIII, assumed control at sixteen years of age in 1902. Uninterested in the daily matters of governing a complex state, the king dedicated himself to the pomp that his office required, overwhelmed by the deteriorating political situation around him.

The young king inherited a worsening economy in an unstable political atmosphere that lacked leadership. Spain's loss of its possessions in Cuba and the Philippines in the war with the United States in 1898 was devastating. The loss of commerce and trade from its colonies dealt a severe blow to its economy and to its self-esteem and prestige. Its place in the international theatre was significantly reduced and ridiculed. A national sense of outrage and depression gripped its people. Alfonso's complete disregard and ability to deal with the complicated circumstances that surrounded him in such a complex time left the country floundering.

Spain was in chaos, divided between two groups with deep philosophical differences. The working class was restless and desperate to improve their condition while the rich opposed any change. There was little doubt that something ominous was about to happen as the spheres of discontent spread through the entire nation.

The political face of Europe was changing. The Great War of 1914 had left Europe in shambles. The nearby success of the Russian Revolution gave birth to a new political philosophy that was quickly gaining favor throughout the rest of Europe and threatening the existing established regimes. Although Spain had remained neutral throughout the war, the influence of the new Communist politic struck a special chord here and it quickly spread within its borders. Spain's long history of worker strikes and liberal activism constantly clashed with the conservative establishment that consisted mainly of rich landowners. This unstable postwar climate set the scene for a monstrous civil war that would decide Spain's future for years to come.

The Spanish Left was comprised of Socialists and Anarchists who had a lengthy history of organizing industrial and skilled workers in the northern cities, particularly the Catalan city of Barcelona. The highly organized agricultural workers demanded better wages and fomented strikes throughout the latter part of the nineteenth century. Their major successes were in southern Andalucía and in Barcelona. The radicalism of the newly formed Communist party injected a vibrant new force that demanded immediate improvement of working conditions. They provoked the workers and labor syndicates in the north to rebel against their condition. These demands were resisted by the owners and the subsequent strikes led to violence along with a severe reaction by the government.

The rich landowners, industrialists and monarchists had always controlled Spain's economy aided by the military. Any need for social change was not recognized nor responded to by this privileged cadre of reactionaries.

The Catholic Church wholeheartedly sided with this faction, fearing its loss of influence over the extremely religious populations that it had exerted unchallenged hegemony over for centuries. The families of wealth controlled the Spanish population with a simple formula that was time worn and assured its influence. Its supremacy and perpetuity sprang from heredity within the wealthy Spanish family. Simply put, one son of privilege—never a woman—entered the military, another the priesthood, and the last the family business. These three vocations, the roots of Spain's high society, guaranteed their continuous rule over Spanish life.

The army officers from this privileged elite felt increasingly uneasy as they watched the chain of events and lack of stability unfolding throughout their country. Their confidence with their king was waning as they saw him unable to find solutions for the country's woes. Spain's poor population had little opportunity, meager education, and few public services. Aside from the few cities in northern Spain, the Spanish economy came primarily from the output of the great land-owners who oversaw the agrarian economy. Peasants were tied to the land as indentured servants.

Spain's atmosphere was gloomy. Unemployment climbed, strikes were called daily and the army became greatly discredited following a disastrous drubbing in a decisive battle in Spanish Morocco where Spain's presence had been secure for centuries.

Finally, in 1923, a career army general, Miguel Primo de Rivera, decided to fill the vacuum left by poor leadership. He seized power in a coup, suspending the authority of the constitutional monarchy—leaving the king powerless. He assumed complete control of all branches of Spanish government. The general quickly revealed himself to be a ruthless dictator, suppressing the striking workers with brutal force. His forces unleashed their weapons and wrath on the working population, killing indiscriminately. Of course, the traditional seats of Spanish power: the oligarchy, the Military and the Catholic Church supported him enthusiastically.

The World Depression of 1929 jolted Spain especially hard. The already impoverished people felt this impact even more. People's discontent and poor living conditions worsened and public order became more difficult to maintain. Students joined workers in the cities and banded together to demand immediate action. They called for more rights, more freedom and for better pay and working conditions.

The circumstances continued to worsen as the military became increasingly disillusioned and alarmed with Rivera's leadership and inability to quell the dissatisfaction. They forced the dictator to leave the country in 1930, naming yet another general to assume leadership of the country. The new general, Damaso Berenguer, could hardly quell the dissatisfaction that he encountered. The country was like a ship without a rudder being pulled in many directions. Berenguer promised to restore the constitutional process and hold general and municipal elections.

Republicans, Socialists and Catalans ignoring the authority of General Berenguer decided to act unilaterally and formed a provisional government completely disregarding his authority. Cataluña, with its industrial city of Barcelona had for centuries resented the interference of Madrid in its affairs and economy and was a constant thorn in the side of Madrid's centralized authority. Berenguer reacted to this defiance by immediately jailing the leaders of this upstart coalition.

A rapid succession of events quickly followed that further confused the political situation. A military coup unhappy with the unfolding events tried to usurp power. Its leaders were caught and quickly executed. Bewildered, General Berenguer resigned. The provisional government was released from jail and moved quickly to promote new, free municipal elections.

From this debacle The Second Republic was born in 1931. The young king Alfonso, bowing to the growing popular demands for democracy and with little military support, refused to abdicate but found no other alternative but to flee Spain for Rome.

The election results that followed were skewed. The monarchists and great landowners were winners in the countryside and the Socialists in the cities. The new government formed in this fledgling republic quickly adopted a new constitution, granted women's rights and allowed Cataluña its autonomous rights once again. A parliamentary and presidential system was established.

The new government was constantly confronted by the coalitions of the right in the congress who opposed any efforts to democratize Spain, fearful of losing its age-old grip of power. The situation worsened and became increasingly more tense and untenable. The Depression worsened as well. Jobs were lost as demands for goods lessened and people suffered desperately searching for any means to survive. The government felt pressed to impose martial law in an attempt to maintain order.

It was decided that new elections should be called and they were conducted in the latter part of 1933. The coalitions of the right won majority control and leadership of the government within the newly formed parliament. Instantly it began to rescind any rights and autonomies previously granted to regions and workers by the former provisional government.

The mineworkers of Asturias in northern Spain reacted resentfully, arming themselves in opposition to the new edicts and taking control of many cities and factories. They burned churches and government buildings and declared themselves autonomous of any central rule. The government's immediate answer was to send armed forces to reassume control of these northern territories in 1934. The combined forces were under the command of General Francisco Franco. Franco was ruthless despite his diminutive stature. He was barely five feet tall. Thousands of workers were killed or jailed. The upstart revolt was quickly and brutally halted.

Political and labor unrest continued. In 1936, due to improprieties in the previous elections in various regions, new elections were called for once again to assuage the populace's demand for change. This time the winner was a coalition of centrist and leftist parties. They were called the Popular Front. They moved immediately to separate the Church from the state and greatly reduced the influence of the rich, rewarding workers with more rights, suffrage for women and equal wages in the working place. These changes would not be long lasting.

The unrelenting hatred by the conservative ruling class and the Church for the new Republican regime or Popular Front lent little hope that anything but conflict would solve solve Spain's internal problems. The united left and moderate factions were equally unwilling and steadfast in their refusal to return to the status quo. They refused to relinquish any of their newly gained rights. Their hatred of the oligarchy, the ruling class, matched that of those who opposed them. All pieces were now in place for a bloody encounter.

The conflict finally started in July of 1936, after a prolonged period of political assassinations from both the left and right. As tensions peaked and cooperation all but nil, no alternative to Civil War was at hand. The insurrection started with Spanish troops stationed in Morocco who crossed over to southern Spain and quickly secured the Port of Cadiz, followed by Sevilla, and then Granada. The war would last three years and hundreds of thousands of people would die. Tens of thousands were imprisoned and many more summarily executed without trials or due process. Thousands left the country, including the Republican leaders, most intellectuals, artists, and free thinkers.

The majority of the military sided with the conservative insurrection and assured its ultimate victory. The Italian fascist government of Benito Mussolini sent thousands of Italian troops into Spain to support his fascist allies. The Nazi air force of Hitler's Germany also sided with the Military. Germany had found a perfect place to test the superior weaponry of its air force on the Spanish populations.

The reluctance of the United States, France and Great Britain to join in the war on the Republican side sealed the fate of the new republic. There was a growing international fear that the increasing radicalism of the Spanish Communists and Anarchists, who sided with the Republican government in Spain, was a child of the Bolshevik revolution of Russia. Their influence was suspect. It was not to be permitted.

Spain was now firmly in the grip of the army, the aristocracy and the Church. Their new leader was the same diminutive general Francisco Franco who led the Moroccan troops, the same man who put down the rebellion in Asturias. He would consolidate his authority and rule for the next forty years by the Grace of God, the inscription he had coined on all Spanish money.

Federico García Lorca, age thirty-eight, poet and playwright, was one of the many dead and missing.

# CHAPTER 4

C ARLOS LOOKED UP, unaware of the time that had elapsed while taking in all he had read. He sat back in his seat and wiped the sweat from his brow. His head felt as if it might explode, and he could not read another word. A mountain of books surrounded him, some half-open and others that would have to wait for another day. His head was swimming with images. Spain's past had jumped out at him and its cast of characters he had been studying flashed before his eyes. Reclining with his eyes closed, he thought deeply about the war.

But his primary question still remained unanswered. Why did they kill Lorca? He came to understand that thousands on both sides were killed—many of those for no good reason. People were summarily executed for the most absurd reasons. And many were killed simply because of people they knew or relatives that fought on one side or the other. Carlos realized that war had few good excuses for so much death and destruction. But why a famous young poet so detached from politics would be executed so quickly at the beginning of the war was incomprehensible to him. The books never conclusively described what Carlos really was seeking, while instead offering a variety of well-worn reasons for Lorca's murder. Most interpretations ro-manticized his death, from which the city of Granada sought to derive great advantage. Images of Lorca were everywhere. Postcards show-ing him as a young man were sold on every corner. As such, Lorca had become a tourist attraction. What irony, Carlos thought; the city that had brutally murdered a favorite son now depended so much on him.

The library in which Carlos sat was a 16th century stone building built in the same period as the *Catedral Central*, the central cathedral in downtown Granada. The narrow streets located behind the cathedral, built by Queen Isabel and King Ferdinand—*Isabela y Fernando*—are the oldest passageways through the city. The remains of the great mon-archs lie in the Chapel at the cathedral's side.

The heat inside the great reading hall continued to be oppressive, despite the presence of small electric fans that had been strategically placed near each reading table. These long rows of tables, almost fully occupied by other patrons, were set tightly together, only adding to the discomfort. Stacks of books were strewn in front of all those who for some reason or another had chosen to challenge the heat of a summer's day by venturing into this "inferno" of learning.

Carlos' thoughts jumped back to the poet. That Lorca was mur-dered here in his hometown of Granada was certain. But why did it happen here of all places? After all, his fame was made while he lived in Madrid. Carlos returned his attention to the books he had withdrawn from the shelves. Perhaps they contained some clues buried between their covers that might offer some compelling reason, but something deep inside fueled his nagging doubt that he would ever find what he was seeking. He sensed the real answers were instead here in the city, hidden among the streets of Granada.

It was just too hot to do any more today. He leaned back, gazing at the walls of the old library and the great curved windows that provided most of the light for the old building. He scanned past the rows of bookshelves that reached almost four meters high at the rear of the high-ceilinged reading room. Old wooden ladders with black wheels creaked along the waxed wood floors, regularly breaking the silence of the quiet room. They reached up to the highest shelves of the tall bookcases as arms to the sky. Carlos shared his long table with several university students whose heads were buried in their work and who seemed oblivious either to their surroundings or the heat. He fanned himself with a notebook, recognizing with some resignation that all his days here were going to be uncomfortable. The fans offered little relief, blowing only more hot air in his face. Carlos quickly concluded that he would have to start in the early morning, before the heat of day could permeate the thick walls of the library. For this, he would need to enter the moment the library opened if he were to productively study without succumbing to the heat.

*The Biblioteca de La Universidad de Granada,* Granada's oldest library and one of its first colonial structures, contained without question the best collection of historical volumes. It was said that the Biblioteca surpassed even Madrid's grand library in its number of volumes dealing with Spain's civil war. The oldest editions—the ones Carlos thought would be particularly helpful—were located on the highest shelves where, naturally, the heat was almost suffocating. They were forgotten relics seemingly banished to their present location—hidden away like so many memories of the tragic Civil War. He often wondered if these volumes were placed as they were—just out of reach—as if to subtly suggest the history he was seeking was also beyond his grasp.

Carlos had always been fascinated with the fact that many of the Spanish poets had studied Spanish literature in the States and South America. But Lorca pulled at him differently—perhaps because he shared with the dead poet a tremendous love for the Alhambra and Gypsy music. He found himself recalling how Lorca had held a great concert in the Alhambra in 1922 featuring many of the best *Cante Jondo* performers of Andalusia. He also wondered if it might be Lorca's tragic ending that lent to this inexplicable infatuation with the poet. Or, was it that both their families had come from Granada? To him it did not matter—the connection existed and as such, Carlos finally found himself in the great city, eager to learn as much as he could.

Carlos leaned back in his chair and stretched. His build was tall and thin, with dark complexion and straight black hair combed back from his forehead. He possessed piercing dark eyes and his sharply defined nose, which he inherited from his Italian mother, gave him a classic Roman profile. Just beneath, his thin lips were pressed together in determination. He found it difficult to spend long hours in the wooden straight back chairs of the library and left his seat frequently to venture outside its entrance to buy bottles of water from a street vendor camped outside. Students gathered around the vendor, laughing and smoking while taking a welcome break from the inferno they and Carlos shared.

Carlos' mind began to race back to how he had arrived in this place. He daydreamed of his great grandfather, a Spanish conscript sent to Cuba somewhere around 1860. In those days, a person of wealth could arrange to have his obligatory military service assumed by a person of lesser means—in exchange for satisfying his debts, providing closure for cloudy legal problems, or through a variety of other ways. The option his great grandfather had chosen was unclear to his family but he was certainly of humble origin—a farmer from Andalusia. Arriving in Cuba, he had become so enamored by the opportunity in and beauty of his new country that he sent word back to his nephew in Spain that Cuba was a place where one could enjoy a better life, in contrast to the hard rigors of Andalusia.

What happened next still remains uncertain to most of the family, but upon the nephew's arrival in Cuba he fell instantly in love with his uncle's wife, who was many years his senior. Such relationships were strictly forbidden—especially in the archaic and rigid society of late nineteenth-century Catholic Spain.

As one might expect, the nephew's stay was consequently cut short, as his uncle's wife found herself with child, pregnant by her newly-arrived lover. She and the nephew were quickly spirited back to Spain, much to the family's chagrin and embarrassment.

Carlos thought it extraordinary that this was the family history his American relatives always recounted. He found himself smirking while thinking of his Spanish family, who in contrast never seemed willing to discuss the matter—leaving unsaid anything and everything that might help clarify this vexing family relationship.

Carlos' great-grandfather remained in Cuba with his seven grown children, one of whom was Carlos' paternal grandfather. Eventually, his grandfather would immigrate during the early part of the century to the United States, where he worked in a cigar factory in the Cuban enclave of Tampa, Florida. He brought with him his wife, a Cuban woman of Canary Islands descent—where, coincidentally, the best Spanish cigars were made from tobacco brought to Africa from the New World. She worked tirelessly at her husband's side for their entire lives, cutting and rolling tobacco in the cigar factories of Ybor City, the Spanish-Cuban barrio of Tampa where, at its peak, over one hundred cigar factories operated at the turn of the twentieth century. Here they raised their family, also having seven children. They returned often to Cuba, which was just a short overnight boat ride from southern Florida. Conveniently, passage was cheap and easy to obtain at a time when neither passports nor other official documents were required for travel between the two countries.

To break the monotony of so many hours seated while rolling cigars, the factory owners brought in *leidores*, or readers, who spent long hours reading Cervantes, the newspapers, and all other varieties of reading materials to educate, inform, and offer something of a diversion for workers engaged in such tedious and monotonous work.

His grandfather would soon encounter troubles of his own when he became involved with the nascent union movement led by Samuel Gompers, the first union organizer to materially improve workers' conditions. Consequently, he was forced to quickly leave the Florida peninsula for New York following a deadly altercation with a strikebreaker.

At about this time, the Cuban-American factory owners decided to lock the cigar makers out of their factories, refusing to allow them to work. Subsequently, unable to sell their tobacco as a result of the chaos of the First World War, the factory owners dismissed their workers for lack of sales. This was the spark that started the worker revolt.

The family was now divided into three branches: the Cuban-Floridian New Yorkers, the family remaining behind in Cuba, and the Spanish Andaluces. It would be more than fifty years before the family would finally reunite—when Carlos' parents established contact with their relatives in the small village of Jete, in southern Granada, Spain.

Cuba later became taboo with America as the country moved to the left with the ascent of President Fidel Castro and his communist revolutionaries in 1959. Travel was no longer permitted between the two nations. Carlos' grandparents could no longer travel freely to and from Cuba, as had been their long time habit. They now looked to Spain to renew ties with the Andaluz relatives and this ultimately provided the backdrop for Carlos' introduction to Granada.

Carlos peered at the old clock above the library's entrance door and, wiping his brow, took notice of the late hour. He was ecstatic he was here and felt very much at home in Granada. He knew the library would be his ally in his quest—affording him access to all the documents essential to his completing this complicated research mission. There were hundreds of histories, biographies, academic critiques of Lorca's works, and scores of magazines that stoked the fires of doubt surrounding the author's capture and the events leading up to his death. There were maps of Granada's environs as well as landmark locations in the city the poet once frequented, which merited visiting. He would have to search determinedly for them amid the thousands of books in the five-hundred-year-old Biblioteca. It made him dizzy when he considered the task before him.

He would certainly have to visit the Huerta de San Vincente, Lorca's family's summer residence, located within Granada, where Lorca had spent the last few weeks of his life. That would be enormously helpful in allowing him to get a feel for the poet. To feel his emotions was crucial to Carlos' task.

Flipping through his notes, Carlos reviewed what he had garnered so far about Lorca's last few days. Sadly, there was little new information he was previously unaware of. Although he was intimately familiar with Lorca's plays and poetry, the events leading up to the poet's death were diluted so as to only add doubt to the mystery. All accounts ended up in the same place — nowhere. It was well-known that Lorca had been whisked away and killed within days of his capture. But no clear picture managed to emerge as to why. Carlos was determined to investigate all questions for which he could not find proper answers. The topic of Lorca's disappearance increasingly seemed to be buried along with the thousands either dead or unaccounted for during the long reign of the dictator Franco.

He folded up his notepads, satisfied overall with the day's endeavors — assuring himself that that he would soon uncover something new; some new clue that did not fit within the standard accounts of the poet's disappearance.

Carlos stood up, stretched, and headed toward the exit, leaving through the tall wooden doors and into Granada's oppressively hot streets. Walking slowly away, he ventured toward his hotel, reciting to himself events in the brief life of the great Granadino poet.

# CHAPTER 5

*Alhambra, al Qa'lat al Hamra, 'red fortress' in Arabic, is the mistress
of Granada, for her shadow falls on all those who live in the city below
and her memory records silently everything she has witnessed.*

AN ENCOUNTER on a hot, humid summer day in the Albayzin is where Carlos' story truly began. The events of that day would change his life. Without this chance encounter, all of Carlos' efforts to succeed in knowing more about Lorca's past would amount to nothing. Crossing the stone bridge over the Rio Darro into the Albayzin, Carlos turned right and started walking uphill toward the caves of *Sacromonte*, in the hills next to the Albayzin. He watched the barkeepers closing up after another long night of song and dance. The streets were empty, as was usual for the early morning. Granada is not a city that begins at morning's early hour. The best *Flamenco* and *Zambra*—the dance of the *Flamenco*—are found here, so Carlos wondered where he might go this hot summer evening to listen to these original and organic sounds of Granada. The tourist sites abounding in the lower neighborhoods closer to the central city and big hotels held little interest for him. If it could be found it would be found here in the Albayzin in the caves. They comprise the center of the original old city that sat below the Moorish fortress where merchants and ordinary people lived and conducted their daily lives while observing all the customs of their predecessors.

Dug into the sides of the surrounding mountains next to the river Darro, these white Gypsy caves are centuries old, serving as homes, bars and stores, and are quite a sight to see—many with TV antennas perched atop their white, rounded roofs. These structures from a prior era operate as if time had stopped and separated them from the modern city of Granada situated below. From this historic compound emanate the Gypsy sounds and music that continue to give beauty, meaning, and rhythm to this ancient city.

Moving upward along the narrow *Paseo*, he noticed a lanky, slender, older man outside a whitewashed cave, seated in an old metal chair with legs stretched underneath. He appeared worn out, tired and unshaven. He was smoking what appeared to Carlos to be a handmade cigarette that lacked dimension, and was watching Carlos as he approached. His long and wiry black hair had traces of gray, which lent him a vibrant look. His big, black, almond-shaped eyes—Gypsy eyes—stayed fixed on Carlos, who returned his stare with a smile. The cave was a *Flamenco* cave, probably just closing, thought Carlos. The old man with the ruddy skin must surely be a Gypsy, Carlos thought. As Carlos passed closer, the man called out, *"As llegao muy temprano o muy tarde"* ("You are either a lot early or a lot late.")

His thick Andalusian accent was difficult to understand. The Andaluces are known throughout Spain for the way they speak—dropping consonants and vowels and tying words together, making it probably the most difficult Spanish in all of Spain to comprehend. It is also the region of Spain located entirely within the country's southern half, where the people are the most poorly educated. Carlos listened intently, struggling to grasp the man's meaning despite his own command of the language. The old man sat looking at this new arrival, drawing heavily on his cigarette. A cloud of smoke enveloped him, as the hot heavy air of the day did not allow it to move away.

*"Para que?"* ("For what?") Carlos answered.

"The caves, music, excitement, the *Zambra* dance . . . all the reasons a young man like you would have to be here."

Carlos looked at him smiling, still straining to comprehend the old man's disconnected speech.

Carlos spoke slowly, "For me, there is no greater time of day than the early morning with its empty streets to stroll around the Alhambra and the Albayzin. It fills me with all its energy, and carries me to another time."

Carlos worried about his response, wondering to himself if his answer had been appropriate — if that was the *real* reason why he was here. He studied the old man, whose interest clearly was piqued. There was something about the old man's presence that was captivating, his eyes that remained fixed on this newcomer he did not know.

"And what do you feel about this place and energy, as you call it?" as smoke poured out from the old man's mouth.

A little taken aback with such a pointed question, Carlos hesitated a moment before answering, but just as quickly realized there was no malice intended. He had not really spoken to anyone in the city who had questioned him since his arrival. Carlos began to explain as the old man kept his gaze steadily on him.

"I sense the Moors, their presence here is so strong ... the flow and grace of this city ... the ghost of the great poet Garcia Lorca that haunts this city almost as if he were still alive. His poetry and descriptions of his beloved Granada still hang in the air, but most of all I love the great music that had its birth here and the sadness of its sound that I see every day in the faces of the people."

The old man eyed Carlos up and down with a serious look, and then a broad smile spread across his ruddy face, revealing a row of tobacco stained teeth.

"You know of Lorca?" he questioned.

"Very much so," Carlos reflexively answered. "I know that his life ended here in this city he loved. I don't understand why he was brutally murdered. That is one reason for my visit and, of course, to enjoy the music of the city, the *Cante Jondo, Zamba,* and *Flamenco.*"

The old man gave Carlos a penetrating stare as if to take full measure of this stranger before him. The heat of the early morning signaled yet another sweltering day to come. He said nothing as he stared intently at Carlos, who felt uneasy until the old man broke the silence, easing his discomfort.

"The morning is a poor time to have a conversation and a poor time to know the monte," the old man said, using the everyday term for *Sacromonte*, the sloping hills above the Albayzin. He motioned for Carlos to take a seat.

Carlos moved around one of the two small, empty metal round tables and chairs before him and sat. The Gypsy sat at the other. Half-full wine glasses, leftovers from the previous evening, were on the tables. The Gypsy pushed aside two full ashtrays and some tourist pamphlets resting near Carlos. He then slid his pouch of tobacco across the table gesturing to Carlos. Carlos declined by shaking his head, while his new acquaintance began to roll a new cigarette with the jet-black tobacco he scooped from the small, black pouch.

The air hung heavy and the situation seemed awkward. For want of beginning a conversation, Carlos began commenting about the quiet morning, the beauty of the surroundings, and the haunting visage of the Alhambra staring down at them. The Gypsy sat quietly, dragging heavily on his cigarette. A young woman with long, black hair emerged from the cave and offered coffee to the old man without even glancing toward Carlos. She was dark complected, tall, thin, and glided toward the two men with a flash in her large and piercing black eyes. Her comely olive skin and broad smile caught Carlos embarrassingly off-guard as he found himself staring at her. She moved as gracefully as a dancer, with lithe arms and long, slender fingers tipped with nails painted a bright red. She disappeared almost as soon as she appeared, returning but a few moments later with a small tray holding two black coffees. She served the old man first with much deference and slow, deliberate motions before turning to Carlos, who thought he noticed her slipping a small smile in his direction. She then retreated into the cave's narrow entrance. She was entrancing and disarmed Carlos completely, causing him to blush. He felt foolish. The Gypsy must have sensed his awkwardness in the moment.

"My daughter Nadya," the old man said.

Carlos immediately relaxed, thankful the old man had come to his rescue. He continued talking, still feeling silly at his reaction to the beautiful Gypsy girl. He talked, or more probably babbled, about the first things that came to his mind: the hot morning; the lack of rain, for it was the dry season in Granada; the dry river bed and the tourists; or saying either nothing or anything to regain his composure.

At this time of year, Granada was besieged by thousands of tourists who had mostly traveled there to see the Alhambra — the *Taj Mahal* of Granada. How the *Granadino*s could accustom themselves to this constant invasion, Carlos commented as the old man sipped his coffee, was remarkable.

The old man then replied, "They come for the same reason as you, the Alhambra, the music, the history . . . this is how we make our living, so the tourists to us are a welcome sight.

"I rarely see anyone walking at this hour who seems to be enjoying himself so much. You appear to take great interest in what you see."

"Interest?" Carlos responded.

*"El pasao,"* ("The past") he remarked in his Andaluz argot. Carlos, confused, sat staring at him.

"The past?"

The old Gypsy did not answer but just smiled again, drawing on his cigarette, and carefully examining the young man before him.

The two sat quietly for several minutes more, gazing upward at the looming Alhambra and at the emptiness of the morning streets that would soon be filled with tourists and noisy automobiles on their way to work.

The Gypsy finally rose from his chair, placing his hand on Carlos' shoulder.

"Why don't you come and visit us for an *espectaculo* tomorrow evening," — it was the Gypsy term for a *Flamenco* performance.

Carlos was thrilled with this unexpected invitation. He was ecstatic at the prospect of watching good *Flamenco*, and to perhaps even catch another glimpse of the Gypsy's beautiful daughter. He also enjoyed the old man's company and looked forward to more conversation with him. Carlos then smiled, glad that he had ventured up into the *'monte'* at this unreasonable hour.

*"Estupendo!"* ("Fabulous!") was his rapid reply.

With a half grin, the Gypsy lit yet another cigarette and continued, "The Alhambra has many stories," adding he would be glad to share some "Stories of Granada and stories of Gypsies."

As the Gypsy suggested, Carlos agreed to return at ten-thirty the following evening, his eyes beaming in excitement at his new found good luck.

*"Como se llama, Señor?"* ("What is your name, Señor?") Carlos asked.

"Neftali," he answered — a Gypsy name.

Carlos, rising from the table, introduced himself as well, and thrust out his hand toward his new friend. The Gypsy shook it and then exited by pushing aside the curtain at the cave's entrance, leaving Carlos alone again in the street. Carlos called out to the old man as he disappeared into the cave, *"Hasta mañana, Señor, y muy buenos dias."* ("Until tomorrow, and a very good morning to you sir.")

Carlos' voice followed the old man into the cave. A smile broke across his face as he turned and continued up the hills of the *Sacromonte,* thinking about the beautiful Gypsy girl and wondering about Garcia Lorca and what kind of life he had lived, surrounded by such beauty.

# CHAPTER 6

Federico García Lorca was born in Fuente Vaqueros, Andalucía, the southernmost region of Spain in 1898. His father, a wealthy landowner, grew sugar beets, which made him handsome profits since Spain's loss of its rich colony, Cuba, to the United States in the disastrous Spanish American War. Spain depended heavily on its colony for the sugar cane that supplied the needs of its country and Cuba was its major port of entry into all of South America. Federico's father, an astute businessman named Don Federico Garcia Rodriguez, anticipated this loss, switching his crops to sugar beets to satisfy urgent demands for sugar. He was a businessman who was well ahead of his time. He had bought the first tractor that Granada had ever seen to work his lands previously tilled by harnessed mules.

Federico, his first-born son, was a sensitive and exceptional individual. As a child, he seemed to understand the death and sadness his family endured when his newborn baby sibling died shortly after childbirth. Federico was only two years of age and the deep sorrow of his family made his small body shake. He sat and cried uncontrollably as his mother attempted to console him. His mother Vincenta, a schoolteacher, loved music and was a gifted pianist. She sensed the special needs of her son who shared her love for music. A gramophone filled their home with the sounds of Andalucia, its *Flamenco* and *Cante Jondo*. The great classical composers Beethoven, Chopin, and Bach could always be heard echoing from inside the family's living room, and neighbors often stopped to listen to the sounds that vibrated the hills near their home. Vincenta shared this gift of music with her first born son eagerly. Federico always preferred to sit and listen to music rather than play children's games as was the case with most of his playmates. The young Federico devoured every musical morsel, showing much talent and appreciation for playing the piano himself and inventing his own songs—always accompanying these creations with his small hands on the piano while singing his invented lyrics. He loved to perform.

He enjoyed creating his own plays and built himself a small stage where he enlisted the family's hired help to participate in his small productions. Many of his schoolmates scoffed at his soft manner. He moved with a quirkiness and awkwardness that his classmates ridiculed, and his tendencies were soon seen as effeminate and gentle.

When his family moved to Granada, the capital of the province of the same name, Federico studied music and spent hours with his mother and music teachers improving his gift for the piano. He played all the Andalusian songs his mother had taught him. He read about Andalucia and studied its literature, its music, its *Flamenco* and its past with little concern for the normal studies required of him.

At his father's bequest, he agreed to study law at the University. Federico's father thought it a practical and worthy profession for a young man of stature to study. He was not an admirer of the arts as his son or wife but always relented at the urgings of Federico's mother. Federico was a terrible student and the law was of little interest to him, but he continued to study—not wanting to challenge the wishes of his father. Don Federico was an able and sturdy man more interested in farming and real estate."

Federico much preferred to pass his time playing the music of

Beethoven, Schuman, Liszt, and the ballads of Granada. He performed recitals at the University with such feeling and intensity that many who heard him took note and marveled at the young man's compassion. Federico saw the world around him as sad and inexplicable. He expressed his feelings at the piano to the delight of his teachers who saw in their student a special quality that was beyond his years. Federico basked in this attention and newly-found notoriety his talent had brought him.

He was awkward in stature and moved about in a clumsy manner due in part to his having been born with one leg shorter than the other, which seemed incompatible with his own body. In spite of, or perhaps because of this, he craved to be accepted and loved by everyone. He was the first to make a joke, to poke fun at some absurdity. The slightest criticism or unkind remark easily hurt his feelings and he would brood for hours or sometimes days over the most insignificant and least intended comment.

But whenever he sat at the piano he became transformed. Whether playing music or reciting composed verses and poems, he was a very different person — more confident and self-assured. He assumed a bravado and flamboyance that assured his being the center of attention. He put on a coat of arrogance like a knight suiting up in armor. When performing, his self-esteem grew. He thrived when he felt appreciated and when his admirers and friends warmly received him. However, he also knew there was a hidden Federico that he could not dare reveal, the sullen Federico of insecurity and doubt.

Despite his poor showing at the university, he remained an avid reader and enjoyed losing himself in the works of the great novelists and poets. He eagerly read the French writer Victor Hugo, the Spanish Ruben Dario, as well as Miguel de Cervantes, author of the immensely popular *Don Quixote*. Lorca imagined himself a modern Quixote — not fighting windmills, but rather by opposing all the strict norms that contemporary Spanish prose and poetry imposed. He felt that Spain was trapped in old ideas and wanting for the appreciation of new ideas. To Federico, Spanish society was stiff and unimaginative—having forgotten all the greatness of its rich history.

Federico marveled at the natural beauty of Granada that surrounded him and saw nature as the custodian of true meaning. He was at home listening to its sounds, spending many hours in the fields and *vega*s at his country home in Asquerosa.

However, the dark side of Federico always lingered within him and revealed itself in his outlook toward the world all about him. He was unable to reconcile the reality of nature—its creation and death that he felt always ongoing around him. In Federico's world, death always loomed nearby. He was always wary in anticipating his own death, fearful that it would call at a moment's notice. He even rehearsed his own funeral as his young friends carted Federico around Granada in a wooden funeral box where he lay with his eyes closed and arms folded on his chest.

In addition to the constant discomfort he endured with his leg, he also felt himself an outcast. Despite his dress, which as a young man usually consisted of a trim suit, collared shirt and tie, Federico cared little about money and most mundane things. Federico's family was wealthy, but he detested the fact that most of his friends and peers could not afford what his family was able to provide for him. He was spoiled and privileged and always the object of his doting mother.

He was most happy in the company of a few select friends who met regularly at *El Rinconcillo*, (the small corner), in the rear of Alameda cafe. They would discuss the great writers, argue about politics, and read and sing to each other. They ridiculed *Granadino* society with its staid ways, its newspapers and thoughtless magazines while drinking coffee and wine. In this setting, Federico was a shining star. He was known for his constant, unexpected outbursts and other eccentric behavior. His whole body shook with passion when he uttered his ideas—always waving his hands wildly in the air. Many times he fell into verse or song to express his sentiments and the group would goad him on—enjoying immensely this strange character they loved and adored.

These young men of the tavern sensed that Spain needed to be awakened from a long slumber. Its present ideas were neither exciting nor creative. Society needed to be *challenged*. They spent many long hours discussing the new modern poetry and art that was starting to surface in France, America and elsewhere.

Aside from these few friends, Federico had little enjoyment. A professor, Señor Dominguez Barreta, had seen him perform at the University and recognized the young man's raw talents after hearing him sing an old Spanish ballad. He prodded Federico to study literature further. He invited Federico and several of his classmates to accompany him on a tour of Andalucia. It would be an opportunity for all of them to feel, touch and see Andalucia, their homeland.

"Look and observe nature and the countryside, reflect on its beauty and write everything down you feel," the professor instructed.

Federico had never left home and his parents fretted, as they understood their son's fragility, but allowed him to go when the professor gave them assurances that he would keep a watchful eye on the young man.

Amazed at what he saw and experienced while touring the various provinces of his homeland, Federico enthusiastically jotted down pages and pages of impressions. He would fill the margins of his journal with line drawings of people and objects he saw along the way. The professor was impressed by Federico's style and pleased that his expectations of the young man were being realized.

In fact, the professor thought the impressions so extraordinary that he pushed Federico to compile and organize them for publication. Federico eagerly accepted this challenge, and with his father's financial aid published his first writings. This book comprised a series of poems he called *Impresiones y Paisajes, (Impressions and Landscapes)*. The small book circulated and was received with much acclaim in Granada. The young poet was on his way and his successes began to multiply quickly in his home town.

Federico thought the greatness of Spain was being forgotten and believed that its traditional music should be revived. His love of music compelled him to reintroduce the Gypsy songs of Andalucia to the people of Granada, remembering all the amazing performers he had witnessed in the journey with his professor.

Along with Manuel de Falla, the famous Granadan musician and composer who had heard of Federico's talent and had soon befriended him, Federico presented a huge assembly of *Cante Jondo* and *Flamenco* singers in a great celebration of *Flamenco* and native song at the Alhambra in 1922. What exuberant times the two musicians had wandering through all the small villages of Andalucia and listening to the local people sing the music of Spain's soul. Federico was twenty-four years old.

His professor urged the family to advance the budding poet's talent, which he believed was impossible to do in provincial Granada. He recommended Federico be sent to Madrid to study at the famous *Residencia Estudantil* (Residence of Students), where the center of Spain's cultural elite gathered and where Federico would certainly flourish alongside similar talents.

Federico's parents thought this a terrible idea and worried excessively about their son's ability to cope in the great city, but were assured that he would be looked after and safely find his way there. Federico's father, as always, disagreed, but after much cajoling from his wife, finally relented and furthermore even agreed to finance this adventure. He would thereafter become the sole financier for many of his son's future projects and creations.

Here in Madrid, he truly did flower. Madrid was cosmopolitan. The continuous nightlife of theatre and concerts, and the constant gatherings of friends discussing everything until the early morning hours gave Federico his first sense of belonging.

He spent many long evenings entertaining his colleagues by playing classical pieces or Gypsy ballads on the piano while reciting the lyrics he put to every song. He was a true showman. In the residence he met an unusual young man, the artist Salvador Dali. And another lodger was Luis Buñuel, the notable cinematographer and director. Both became Federico's constant companions, roaming the late hours places until dawn.

Federico also suffered from an internal conflict that caused him great pain. His sexuality became a constant subject of doubt, though he did not reconcile or easily adapt to his latent homosexuality, which Catholic Spain viewed as morally degenerate. Federico detested the effeminate male and joked often of the pretty women he encountered while he discreetly engendered many relationships with male friends. His long relationship with Dali was a subject of gossip among his friends.

Federico wrote and staged many plays and his fame in the theatre travelled throughout Madrid and Spain. His recurrent themes of death and love always involved tragedy, which he saw as the natural state of man. Spanish custom made for great difficulty in accepting anything outside of its rigid understanding of the roles of man and woman. They were cast apart—each within the confines of what was morally acceptable—with the woman always in the subservient position. However, Federico moved outside these limits when he presented these themes in his plays and poetry. He rejected traditional theatre. He moved among the people of the arts, drank and smoked heavily while he worked and wrote continually. The critics both adored and despised him. His colleagues loved him but detested his lifestyle. He was always late, for which he was always ready with excuses, and his appearance seemed at times disheveled. Deadlines and promptness were not part of his makeup. However, once he entered into a room he was the center of attention, the showman, the poet, and the life of the party. He was unstoppable in his singing, reciting, and commenting. Fortunately, his frenetic and clumsy style always seemed to add to the impact of his performance and his unusual look and dress were a magnet to everyone near him. His typical wardrobe consisted of loose fit-ting clothes, a habitual string tie, and floppy coat.

Federico García Lorca, now renowned as playwright and poet, was invited for engagements in the United States and South America as companies in Argentina, Cuba, and the United States performed his plays. Simultaneously, his books of poetry were circulating throughout all of South America and Europe. He would spend wonderful years in New York, Argentina and Cuba, where he performed his works and gave lectures as his celebrity grew.

When he finally returned to Spain, dark clouds were forming as the political situation worsened. Federico, for his part, never belonged to a political party or persuasion. The Civil War of 1936 was about to begin, and he was terrified. At the time, he was thirty-eight years old, and did not feel safe in Madrid. Political assassinations were occur-ring daily. He decided to take refuge in Granada with his family where he thought he would be safe. Granada was the most conservative of the Andalusian cities and Lorca returned, despite warnings from his friends begging him not to abandon Madrid. It was July of 1936.

Shortly after returning, he was arrested without being charged. Retribution from the right was horrific, and hundreds of Republican and syndicate officials were summarily executed. Federico was then taken beyond the outskirts of Granada to the small town of Viznar in August of 1936, where he too was executed. Local lore has it that he was killed for his sexual persuasion—having seduced the son of a local po-liceman, while others maintain that his poetry and plays were morally reprehensible and made a mockery of Spain. In any event, his remains have never been recovered.

# CHAPTER 7

C ARLOS WAS PROUD of his heritage. His was an immigrant family that thrived in its culture. His home was filled with the sounds of Afro-Cuban music — the *Cumbias* of Colombia, the *Sambas* of Brazil. His parents taught him to appreciate the cultures of Spain, Mexico, Colombia, and the Caribbean islands. And they always brought home mementos of their travels — including music and literature. Carlos' father spoke often of their family's history and harped on the importance of maintaining its traditions. He was a big man with a rheumatic heart who cared little for diet and drank in excess. He never entertained thoughts of retirement and died at the age of seventy-four, leaving Carlos to tend to the poorly-managed and maintained family business.

Soon after his father's death, and tiring of the constant demands of a business he did not enjoy, Carlos received some luck that presented the opening he had hoped for — a generous offer was made to purchase it. Carlos, in truth, had never really shared the dreams of his father. He did not have that same love of land or of living in and ruling his own small kingdom. His father planted trees and grew vegetable gardens, but mostly lived to build. He converted an ancient barn into a series of rooms and invited his city friends to pass time with him in the country at his new small inn. Over the years, he acquired more property and built homes for those close friends who wanted to share in his dream.

American cooking seldom entered into the family's daily diet—their preferring instead the Latino meals to which they were accustomed. And although Spanish and English were spoken at home, only English was acceptable in the streets; but the family confidently spoke both without any trace of accent.

Spanish literature was venerated as the family shared a keen interest in the great writers. They read Cervantes' *Don Quixote*, and other great writers of the *Generation of '98*—avant garde Spaniards who dared to question Spain's docile attitude and moral decay after their tragic defeat to the United States in the Spanish-American War of 1898. The family favorites were Unamuno, Otega y Gasset, and Pio Baroja—all writers who were moved to regenerate the flagging spirit of Spain, whose standing in the world had since deteriorated.

Carlos devoured it all and the decision to further his study was natural. He pushed his family to allow him to study abroad and spent a year at the Universidad de los Andes in Bogota, Colombia. Here he was introduced to the works of the great South American writers and thinkers of this century: Octavio Paz, the Mexican poet and diplomat; Pablo Neruda, the poet and politician; Jorge Luis Borges, the great Argentine poet and writer; and a whole new generation of South American writers. He traveled throughout Colombia, visiting the hot and humid cities of Cartagena de Las Indias, Barranquilla, and Santa Marta on the northern coast. He encountered the great inland waterway that connects Cartagena to Barranquilla built by slaves brought from Africa and visited the Tairona Indian tribes in the mountains adjacent to Santa Marta. Carlos marveled at their small stature and tremendous strength. They could ascend the mountains in a matter of hours, whereas it took most people a full day—or more—of travel.

He read about Simón Bolivar, the liberator who lived here, and his struggles to free the country from the grip of Imperial Spain. Hitchhiking to Peru, he took in the great Inca cultures of the highland mountains. Their songs, called *huaynas,* were played mostly with bamboo flutes and drums, and were unlike any sound he had ever heard. It was eerily sad music.

He kept a journal of his impressions during these travels and enjoyed recording what he had seen. He carefully cataloged the notes of his observations, and the people with whom he spoke. As his passion for writing grew, Carlos began to realize that it was his calling.

His parents urged him to visit Mexico and taste its wonderful culture when his studies were finished. They talked of the diversity of that huge country with its Indian cultures, diverse languages and fascinating history. Their enthusiasm both intrigued and motivated him. He packed his bags once again and headed north to Mexico. Carlos wandered through the deserts of Sonora in the North, and down the Gulf Coast in the East—in the process finding what he thought to be a truly remarkable culture in the city of Veracruz. Few Indians lived in this coastal city, which was very much like the Cuba his father had described. There was a large black population here in this historic Spanish port of entry—descendants of slaves brought in by the Spanish conquerors. It reminded his father of Havana and its mulatto culture. He said the rhythm of the two cities was the same—vibrant and fast moving. The city's layout resembled that of the old Spanish port cities of Sevilla, Malaga or Cadiz. Veracruz had a *malecon,* a great avenue running parallel to the sea his father said was very much like that of Havana. White-columned stucco buildings of Spanish design lined the streets facing toward the ocean.

Carlos reveled in the nightlife. The Afro-Cuban sounds of the local music, with their drums and marimbas, were constant and everywhere and defined the daily rhythm of the city—infectious to the point that the local people walked to it. Many an unforgettable evening was spent in the local bars drinking Veracruz rum and listening to the stories of the city. Few tourists frequented the east coast of Mexico, which lacked beautiful beaches and upscale hotels, but proved to be an idyllic location for Carlos to spend days-on-end reading, walking the city, conversing with its inhabitants, and writing his impressions. He spent a hot, humid summer reading the great Mexican writers, bathing in the warm waters of the Gulf of Mexico, and enjoying the Afro-Veracruz cuisine. To Carlos it was a welcome break from the world.

Carlos was fascinated by the Indian influences in this country. The clash of cultures made it difficult to distinguish between what was Spanish and what was Indian. This collision had left even the church unrecognizable. The church rituals were surely not like any Catholic mass the he had ever attended. Indian practices mixed the teachings of the Spanish priests with their own ancient customs. The Indians could easily accept the church as long as they could adapt it to their own concept of God.

He read translations of the great *codices*—hieroglyphic parchments left behind by the indigenous population that revealed their understanding of the universe around them. They were, in many respects, much more advanced than their European conquerors. Their calculations of celestial movements of the Earth, Moon and Sun proved much more accurate than those of the Spaniards. Visiting the ancient ruins of central Mexico and the Great Pyramids of the Mayan Yucatan instilled in Carlos a deep sadness. Those cultures were destroyed by the conquering Spaniards and supplanted by the fanaticism and Catholicism of the invaders. He would later compare the destruction of this culture to the devastating damage suffered by the Moors at the hands of the Spaniards in Spain.

But ultimately, Mexico seemed to lack something that Carlos was intently seeking—refinement.

It was in this spirit that Carlos felt Spain was pulling him—that this was where he should be. A tremendous excitement was starting to build inside him. He was thrilled with the prospect of visiting his family and spending time in Granada—where the poet who was becoming such an integral part of his life, the great Lorca, had been born and had loved so much.

On the Spanish peninsula, Carlos headed immediately to Jete, Granada to reacquaint himself with his relatives. They were farmers who lived uncomplicated lives and rarely left their small town. They were eager to greet Carlos and learn the latest news of their extended family in America. One favorite Spanish aunt, Carmen, would relate to him the family history for hours at a time. She knew the names of every relative, who they married and where they eventually settled — both in Spain and Cuba. She completed in minute detail the sketchy history Carlos' father had related to him. She was also the only one who referred to the episode of his great grandfather. Carlos wished that his father had been able to share these wonderful sessions with him.

Cousin Paco, husband of Esther and Carmen's sister, never missed a day in the campo — the fields — and rarely went to town. Paco was a slight, robust man of great strength and with a smile that filled up his entire face. The family's routines never varied and Carlos was continually amazed at how their children appeared to live similar lives — to follow exactly in their footsteps, and were always very close to their parents. It is this traditional aspect of Spanish life, the closeness of family, that he realized was missing in America.

Carlos traveled throughout the beautiful Spanish peninsula, sleeping at times in open fields with castles perched above him . . . a Don Quixote from a different time living in a dream. He walked the *Camino de Santiago* (The Way of Saint James), the holy Spanish pilgrimage through northern Spain — the same paths that pilgrims have trod for a thousand years. Carlos humbled himself at the tomb of the Apostle Saint James the Great, who was said to have brought the word of Jesus Christ to Spain. He saw the great markets of Zamora, the great stone buildings of Caceres, the *alcazabas* (forts) of Toledo and Sevilla, and sat in awe for hours in the great Moorish *Mezquita* of Cordoba. Carlos dedicated himself to writing, feeling liberated from the responsibilities of work, and listened intently to the sounds of Spain — being quite surprised to hear bagpipes in Galicia and Asturias in northern Spain and to learn that the Celts had arrived and settled there.

The idea that had been taking shape in his head for some time was becoming clearer. The streets and libraries of Granada so near his family were the perfect "classroom" for the work he was about to undertake, during which time he was burdened neither by worries nor time constraints. Carlos was most eager to start work on this new project. He was well versed in Lorca's poetry, the raw themes of his plays, his forceful images and strong passions. Lorca was now his passion. He was dissatisfied with so many contradictory accounts of his death and never could reconcile how such a beautiful young talent could disappear so abruptly and without real motive. That uncertainty was what was pushing him to attempt something different, to perhaps shed new light on those final days in a different way.

A constant preoccupation with, and analysis of his death left everyone in Granada with ambivalent feelings. For many it was old news; painful and rehashed with monotonous regularity. Carlos was often turned away from locals with disdain, as they seemed tired of his constant questions and concern for the poet. It was as if the city, like Lady Macbeth's stain, could never rid itself of the guilt or blame for such a heinous act. Why couldn't they just put it behind them—to let the matter rest once and for all? After all, as many Granadians remarked angrily, hundreds of others had suffered similar fates as Lorca's. His notoriety kept the city's wounds from healing. Some people Carlos spoke with suggested that if Lorca's history had not been so tragic, he would hardly be remembered. His poetry and plays were ordinary to many Spaniards who were exhausted from the constant reworking of his life and death. One man who ran a coffee shop Carlos liked to visit complained that Granada had many poets who were far superior to Lorca.

Carlos thought it strange that despite an antipathy toward discussing both the war and the poet's death, Granada had lured tourists by taking advantage of the poet's fame and demise. As part of this effort, his summer home in the central city had been restored, and a museum was built to honor him. He was now the second most popular attraction after the Alhambra. Daily visits took tourists to the supposed site where he was executed. Symposiums were held in his honor. The Alhambra and Lorca were now of equal value to Granada.

Carlos traveled to *La Huerta de San Vincente*, Lorca's family's summer residence, spending hours in the poet's library and study. Stories were plentiful about the poet's sensitivity. One oft-repeated episode related by a groundskeeper Carlos befriended, was that when Lorca was a small child, he noticed a dead bird in his yard—and had spent the next few days crying constantly while being consoled by his mother. He had always been emotional and fearful of death.

As a young man, Lorca witnessed injustice, pain and hypocrisy in Spanish society. And he expressed his dismay freely through his poetry. As Carlos became more intimately involved in Lorca's state of mind during those confusing times, strange feelings began to wash over him. Granada had lured Lorca back home from Madrid where he did not feel safe. Yet it was the treachery of his own city, a city that could not forgive his talent, that brought about his end. Carlos also felt intuitively that some force had spirited him here and that some unknown destiny awaited him as well.

Had Granada mistaken Lorca's poetry and critical theatre as a condemnation instead of understanding its brilliance and creativity? To Carlos, Lorca's poetry was a gift to Spain and Granada. Yes it was true that it was critical of many things Spanish, but to Carlos it only proved Lorca's love for his country. His *Oda a la Guardia Civil (Ode to the Spanish Civil Guard)* was seen as an unforgivable attack on a pillar of Spanish society—its famed police. Carlos saw it as beautiful lyricism that described, through vivid poetic images, a time in history when the police regularly attacked Gypsies. It was mysterious and worrying to Carlos that a city could have such power over a person. He wondered if it might share some of its dark secrets with him. Or, would Granada spit him out as well?

# CHAPTER 8

THE FOLLOWING EVENING at nine thirty, Carlos exited his hotel room next to the Alhambra. It was a good hotel and relatively new. Its name, *Alixares de Generalife,* was taken from that of the summer residence of a Moorish king of Granada. Carlos walked on the beautiful inlaid marble floor of pinks and reds always painstakingly polished by a team of workmen who took great pride in this daily task. Its director was his longtime friend Joaquin, whom Carlos had met with his cousin Armando from Almuñecar when both young men visited the States as teenagers.

During prior visits, Carlos would stay at the Washington Irving Hotel, a landmark located just down the narrow avenue from the Alixares. The hotel was named after another son of Granada. The American writer and diplomat lived and worked in the Alhambra in 1829 where he wrote the *History of the Conquest of Granada* and *Tales of the Alhambra.* Irving resided at this hotel, which was previously called Siete Suelos (Seven Skies), in Granada before he was given the opportunity by his hosts to relocate to preferred quarters in the Alhambra fortress.

He often imagined Washington Irving sitting alone in his room in the Alhambra, staring down over the city and landscape and spending days penning his history of Granada. Carlos read his copy of *Tales of the Alhambra* and felt envy that as a special guest of the Alhambra he was provided with such privileged accommodations, which no longer is possible. It has been many years since the government of Granada designated this tourist destination a national landmark.

Federico García Lorca also spent much time visiting friends at this hotel. The Washington Irving was the preferred site where travelers chose to stay when visiting the city. The hotel lobby had a grand piano that the poet often played while entertaining his friends with songs and verses. It became the favorite meeting place of all the cultured and educated guests who occasioned the city. Sadly, the hotel had been closed for several years—to Carlos' great disappointment. Its long, narrow and dark halls together with its late nineteenth century architecture and interior design were intriguing. Carlos imagined its famous guests—now keeping watch in oil portraits hanging on the long corridor's walls—as seated on the old baroque tapestry furniture now covered with plastic sheets. Every traveler who stayed there must have felt the grandeur of this extraordinary residence with so rich a history and so near the Alhambra.

The close proximity of the Hotel Alixares to the Alhambra helped assuage Carlos' disappointment at the closing of the Washington Irving. The accommodations on the third floor afforded breathtaking views of the Moorish ruins and its wonderful gardens. This floor was reserved for residences and the small quarters were perfect for a prolonged stay. Carlos managed to quickly adapt to his surroundings and befriended the hotel's courteous staff. At reception was Don Manolo, a slight, dark Andaluz from Castel de Ferro, a small town on the eastern coast near Carlos' family's home in Jete. Manolo was always jovial, and spoke fluent Spanish, French and English. For him, the prospect of retiring, even though it was possible for him to do so at any time, frightened him. "What would I do with myself? I know nothing else," he always remarked.

The three *camareros* (bartenders), have been there since the hotel's opening. In Spain, staff turnover is rare, which finds the same people in the same positions year after year. The name of one barman, Jose Antonio, would immediately connote something odious to those of the political left, for Jose Antonio Primo de Rivera had been the founder of the Falangist party in 1933, which became the party of the infamous dictator Generalissimo Francisco Franco following the Spanish Civil War's end in 1939. Jose Antonio Primo de Rivera, son of the previous dictator, was captured and executed by the Republicans at the beginning of the War. But as it turned out, the name fit the bartender well as he despised the current Socialist government.

Paco and Pepe, the other barmen who worked with him were of the left but despite this, they treated each other amicably and with respect. They continually bantered about the merits of the Socialists and Conservatives. The Civil War, finally won by the Fascists, still caused great friction among many citizens. Its wounds cut deeply and across family lines and so the three barmen preferred not to let Spain's history interfere in their daily routines.

Outside the hotel, Gypsy women with *romero* (rosemary), awaited tourists to tell them their fortunes as they approached the entrances of the Alhambra. They were impossible to avoid, and once the unsuspecting tourist took the rosemary in his hand his fate was sealed. The timid tourists taken by surprise had no alternative but to hear their fortunes and give the Gypsies the pesetas they requested.

Carlos descended the mountain toward his evening appointment, taking the usual tourist route, the *Paseo de los Gomerez*. It is well lighted by tall steel *faroles*—street lamps from the nineteenth century. The *Paseo* exits at the *Plaza Nueva*, passing through a great stone arch built by Carlos V, the grandson of King Ferdinand and Queen Isabella. As the Spanish King, he built a summer residence, the *Palacio de Carlos V* within the walls of the Alhambra. It is a giant stone structure of Renaissance design—a masterpiece of sixteenth century architecture. But despite its beauty, it was out of place—a baroque structure encircled by graceful Moorish edifices that had been constructed in the thirteenth and fourteenth centuries.

Both sides of the *Paseo* are lined with tall, beautiful Sycamore and hard oak trees. Stone trenches conducting constant streams of running water built by the Moors run parallel to this verdant forest walkway and create the most exhilarating and calming sounds imaginable. The water feeds the many fountains that adorn this idyllic passageway to the city below. And the dense canopy of overgrowth overhead restricts sunshine from entering, maintaining the *Paseo*'s coolness during descent—despite the oppressively hot sun of summer. Along the way there is a bronze figure set in a fountain dedicated to Angel Ganivet, the 19th century poet and author. He was a precursor of the Generation of '98 and the first to question Spain's role in the modern world. But he met with a tragic end by drowning himself at the age of thirty-three. Each time Carlos walked down the *Paseo,* he stopped and sat by this statue, thinking of Ganivet and the processions of Moorish and Spanish knights and all those who passed through here centuries before him.

Halfway down the walkway was the *Bilrambla,* the original stone Moorish entrance to the fortress. The forest now hid this seven-meter-tall structure covered with ivy. Carlos envisioned Moors on horseback dressed in colorful regalia entering into their red city through this ancient gate.

The plaza below was a central meeting place in this part of the old city, with a sprawling stone terrace with many bars, small eateries, restaurants and guest hostels. A large fountain graced the middle of this large plaza where pigeons gathered to take a drink or bathe in the clean water. People gathered at all times of the day for coffee, or for a glass of wine or beer and *tapas* before heading home to dine. It was just a short walk east of the narrow bridge Carlos had crossed yesterday. At this time of day, walking up the *Paseo de los Tristes* next to the Rio Darro was a pleasure for Carlos, as the city had heated up with activity. The streets were crowded with people moving in all directions. The *Tristes* was quite narrow and Carlos did his best to avoid all the motor scooters and small diesel cars scooting by and filling the air with a panoply of noises, noxious odors and bursts of black smoke. Carlos watched in awe as whole crowds moved toward their homes in the *Sacromonte* and western parts of the city.

Carlos guessed he would arrive by about ten in the evening, when activities were just beginning to unfold at the cave. He hoped to have enough time to find Neftali and perhaps catch a glimpse of the young, pretty woman he had seen yesterday. He wondered to himself if she might be the real reason he had accepted Neftali's invitation so quickly.

Arriving at the cave shortly past ten, Carlos noticed that the two tables outside were gone. Entering through the cave's narrow entrance, he found himself in a small room with triangular metal lights and adornments hanging from the low ceiling. The white walls curving into the ceiling followed the lines of the cave's contour. Hanging from the ceiling were typical *Granadino* plates and bowls of blue and white, and cooking pans made of shiny polished bronze and copper. Long-handled serving spoons and many varieties of blue, red and white *Granadino* pottery filled the cave. Pictures of dancers and celebrities from both the past and present covered the walls. About twenty straight-back wooden chairs with woven straw seats formed a circle around three sides of the cave's walls. The cave could not have been more than four meters wide and perhaps ten meters in length. A small wooden platform at the room's center, barely raised above the earthen tile floor, was designed for dancing. Five small stools placed in a row occupied the other side of the space. And at one end of the room, a narrow doorway covered by a red curtain appeared to be the entrance to adjoining chambers. This remarkable scene, with its variety of striking colors and shiny objects, was straight out of a glossy tourist guide and dazzling to the eye.

Several tourists were already seated and being attended by two young men in white and ruffled long-sleeved shirts and tight black trousers. Their olive skin and dark, shiny hair suggested their Gypsy heritage. They were serving an aperitif, a glass of red wine, and talking quietly to the newly arrived while collecting the fare for the evening's performances.

Carlos looked around for Neftali and the young, pretty woman but they were nowhere to be seen. He moved to a corner where one of the young servers spotted him and with a quick smile moved to offer the customary welcoming glass of wine.

"*Vino tinto, señor?*" he asked.

"*Claro que si,*" ("Of course") Carlos answered.

"Will you stay for the early *espectaculo* only, *señor?*"

Remembering that *Flamenco* shows or *espectaculo*s were repeated during the same evening—both an early and late show—Carlos replied quickly, "I will stay for both."

"*Son mil pesetas los dos, señor,*" ("That will be a thousand pesetas for both, señor").

Carlos counted out the peseta notes, and waited for the *espectaculo*—Gypsy show—to begin, all the while watching the excitement build on the faces of the tourists. The cave had filled up quickly, with some Spaniards, but mostly tourist visitors who had come to watch *Flamenco*. The lights on the ceilings flickered suddenly and the chatter ceased in anticipation. The red curtain moved aside and a young man dressed like the two servers appeared. He had long, black, wavy, oily hair with olive skin carrying a guitar. Then came an older, stout woman, dressed in a long ruffled dress of blue polka dots. A red braided shawl with long tassels rested across her shoulders. She wore long, gold chains around her neck and matching gold bangles on both wrists. A bright red lipstick contrasted with her olive skin and her hair fell to her shoulders. She was followed a young, slender woman with long, blond hair and similar olive complexion who wore a similar dress but with red polka dots. To Carlos' surprise, he now realized that all Gypsies did not have black hair. Her appearance was complemented by a blue shawl that fell across her well-defined arms and shoulders.

Next came the coffee server of the previous day, in a green dress of polka dots, which revealed her narrow waist and tall, lithe body. Her arms were almost completely ringed with silver bangles, and large silver hoops dangled from her ears, contrasting perfectly with her dark appearance. Her long, graceful nose was situated right above her upper lip. Carlos thought she resembled a Gypsy Cleopatra. She looked straight ahead as if she did not even notice the crowd of people watching her. Carlos felt his heart skipping beats. He had never seen such a beautiful woman and felt himself blushing hoping she would not look his way.

Finally, Neftali entered. He was dressed similarly to the other men, with white ruffled shirt and loose-fitting black slacks with gold embroidery decorating the cuffs. The troupe moved in unison toward the stools and sat down, smiling and looking at one-another—readying themselves for the evening's performance. The cave fell silent.

The Gypsy, Neftali, began to clap his hands rhythmically. This piercing sound slowly filled the cave with its resonance. His smart clapping began to grow louder and faster. After several moments, the guitarist stroked two strong chords, which exploded into the air. Two young dancers—the blond woman and the coffee server—stood up and entered the center of the platform. They stretched their arms above their heads in a slow and deliberate motion with their wrists and fingers slowly gyrating and articulating upward. Their graceful movements were delicate and swan-like. They wore black shoes with thick heels that started to bang out a counter-tempo to the guitar and clapping. Circling each other with arms almost intertwined they spun around and around with enormous energy—their chins tucked into their collarbones while exuding the most stoic of looks. Neither had their eyes fixed on the audience or each other. Occasionally, their hands dropped and grabbed at the pleats of their dresses, their feet tapping in time on the hardwood surface. The guitar's strumming became increasingly louder as the dancers feverishly gyrated from side-to-side, responding to the shouts from their seated comrades—high-pitched commands of encouragement.

Neftali began singing in rhythm with his clapping. The words emanating from his throat resembled gurgling more than melodic intonations. The guitarist's fingers stroked solid, staccato chords while Neftali forcefully clapped and groaned his Gypsy tune.

After several minutes and much fevered exertion, guitar strumming and Neftali's clapping and moaning, the two dancers stopped, suddenly caught in their perfect form, their arms high in the air as Neftali shouted a passionate *"Ay! Ay! Ay!"* Their dance was over.

The audience roared its approval and Carlos found himself shouting along with them as the dancers found their way back to their stools, their skin glistening with perspiration and sharing broad smiles with each other. After an interval of several more minutes, the guitarist and the young blond woman stood to take another turn at the center of the small platform while their companions remained seated. The two young servers took this opportunity to move about the audience, refilling empty wine glasses. The seated trio then began clapping in unison with intermittent shouts and loud exhortations to inspire the dancers. The young male dancer's hands gently traced the graceful lines of his partner's body as she neared him. Her arms were continually extended upward while her wrists and fingers never ceased their circular motion in perfect harmony with the rhythmic clapping that filled the room. And their feet were completely in simpatico, pounding out a similar rhythm against the platform's boards. It radiated an intense sexuality as the pair moved about with their eyes always fixed on each other. They were awarded the same tidal wave of applause from the crowd as they returned to their seats—perspiration running down their faces, as the cave's heat on this summer night was exceeded only by that of the dance.

Next, with the older woman's turn to perform, only Neftali clapped and from his throat emanated the most guttural of sounds. Carlos could not comprehend anything he sang, as his mouth became an instrument—the words vibrating as they left his lips. And though the woman lacked the grace of her younger dancers, she seemed to connect to the voice of Neftali in a instinctive way, moving her body slowly and deliberately while her heels smacked the wooden floor. Her performance was thoroughly captivating, and when she finished, she received prolonged applause from those in attendance who viscerally experienced the fervor of her effort. Shortly afterward, the lights on the walls flickered, marking the end of the first performance after almost an hour and a half.

The audience rose slowly from their chairs and headed toward the doorway. The dancers moved among them, offering thanks for their attendance and inviting them to return soon.

Neftali approached Carlos smiling, *"Te gusto?"* ("Did you enjoy?")

"It was wonderful and you have a captivating voice."

Carlos informed him that he would stay for the second performance as well.

The next *espectaculo* was even better than the first. Whether it was the later hour of the evening or that the dancers were more loose and nimble, their emotions overflowed into the crowd, which was comprised mostly of Spaniards who seemed to have a greater appreciation for the talent before them. At this point in the evening, most of the Albaycin's caves were frequented by the locals. The audience shouted commands and rewarded the dancers with their approval as they actively participated in the performances. Carlos wondered to himself if the locals, knowing tourists would not attend performances this late in the evening, purposely attended the second show. The dancers played more enthusiastically to this appreciative assembly, by prolonging their routines until the audience was as physically and emotionally exhausted as they were. At evening's end, the troupe remained seated quietly on their stools, not mixing with the crowd as they had previously. Carlos moved slowly toward the exit when his coffee-serving dancer approached him.

"My father would enjoy your company for a small meal as soon as all have left. Would you like to join us?"

Of course he would stay. Carlos looked forward to continuing the conversation with Neftali they had begun yesterday. And he knew he would also have another opportunity to get to know better this pretty daughter that disarmed him so completely with her voice and looks.

"I would be pleased to join you," Carlos replied.

*"Como se llama?"* ("What is your name?") he asked.

"Nadya," she replied.

# CHAPTER 9

NEFTALI AND NADYA invited Carlos to sit at a small table that two young men brought from inside the red curtain. Two small plates of *Chorizo* and *Morcilla,* Spanish blood sausage, were served along with a flask of green olive oil and a plate of green peppers with sliced tomatoes and garlic. A large bowl of olives and a basket of warmed bread made for this typical Andaluz meal. A bottle of *rioja,* a favorite Spanish red wine from the Rioja region was served. Carlos' two tablemates began eating heartily discussing their performance while he feasted on olives and bread washed down with the delicious wine.

Neftali raised his head and addressed him while helping himself to a second glass of wine,

"You know we owe our life in music to García Lorca and de Falla who searched the countryside of Andalucia for the sounds of *Cante Jondo.* They went from village to village, listening to the peasants sing their traditional songs. They stopped at bars and cafés and wherever they could to listen to the local versions of this very old form of music. They asked the people they found to come to Granada for a great contest they were planning, to showcase the best of the *Cante Jondo.* This happened on a June weekend in 1922. Lorca was quite a young man with a mission, only twenty-four years of age, when he assembled all those whose music he had heard.

"The event was scheduled to happen in the Alhambra. Without Lorca, I am sure that our songs would not have the place and importance that they do now. He and Falla needed to show Spain the significance of this deep song, this *Cante Jondo*. They recognized the genre, both as the soul and true spirit of their country, and also the need to respect and preserve its traditional singing. The *Flamenco*, was soon being sung throughout Spain, which commercialized the *Cante Jondo*. But it was sung badly, and was just as quickly demeaned and relegated to obscurity—largely removing it from its rightful place in Spanish culture.

"Now, every year in July a festival is held in the Alhambra where the best performers sing the *Cante Jondo* to honor our music and more to honor Lorca and de Falla for their contribution."

"He is one of us," Neftali continued.

"Lorca was a Gypsy?" Carlos asked, surprised.

"No, not of blood, but truly in spirit. He was one of few who understood us. He captured our hearts and souls with his verse and poems. He recognized what we are and shared it with the world, before it could be forgotten. His *Gypsy Ballads*, his poem of Andalucia proved to us that he was one of us. Lorca said, 'the Gypsy is the highest, the deepest, the most genuine, and the greatest aristocrat of my country; also the guardian of the alphabet, the blood and the marrow of the Andalusian truth.'"

Carlos had read and was well aware of Lorca's *Gypsy Ballads*, his *Romancero del Gitano*, the poetry that lifted Lorca to fame in Spain and throughout the world. He remembered the ballads of "The Gypsy Nun" and "The Romance of the Moon" as his favorite verses:

> *Flee, moon, moon, moon. If the Gypsies were to come,*
> *they would make with your heart white necklaces and rings.*

66

"How Lorca was able capture the spirit and soul of the Gypsy in verse was magical," Carlos said.

Neftali sat back in his chair taking out his pouch of tobacco. He sipped his wine while rolling a thin cigarette and looking straight at Carlos.

"May I tell you a little about the Gypsies? I am sure you have heard of our bad reputation—that we are thieves and despise work. For a few of us, that is the truth; but I would say the same for the Spaniards as well. The Gypsies came to Spain in the early fifteenth century, arriving from North Africa—*not* from Eastern Europe, as everyone thinks. We speak *Calo,* which is Andalusian Spanish with our own words mixed in. The *Flamenco* you listened to tonight is a mixture of the Moorish, Arabic, and Sephardic peoples we came in contact with. It comes from *fellah mengu,* f-l-a-m-e-n-c-o, which means 'escaped peasant' in Andalusian Arabic. The strong influence of the Moors that ruled Spain for seven hundred years is something the Spanish should never forget, but they will. We were persecuted, as were the Jews and Arabs. We did not mix but kept to ourselves—keeping alive our traditions. We are no different than perhaps the Chinese, who rarely mix with other races."

Listening intently, Carlos had supposed his evening would be pleasant, but was so delighted to find someone so knowledgeable who appeared to share his same passions. Could it possibly be that he might start his investigations right here in this cave? Did Neftali know more about the dead poet? What a great stroke of luck *that* would be, he thought to himself!

Neftali continued, "We gather here from time to time to sing the old songs, the *Cante Jondo,* the songs of the peasants. It is quite different from what you saw this evening. We invite people we know from the countryside, many who sing in the same style as those who performed at that first concert in the Alhambra. Would you be interested in joining us? I am sure you will enjoy hearing them. I would very much like for you to come."

Carlos was beside himself with excitement and accepted the invitation instantly. He thanked Neftali for sharing the late meal with him and rose to go, shaking his hand.

"Thank you so much," Carlos said, addressing both father and daughter. As Nadya stood also to escort him to the cave's door, Carlos could not help but notice her beauty and how being near her made him feel queasy inside.

"We will call you when we would like to meet next—please let us know  where you can be reached," Neftali said as he stood up and disappeared behind the red curtain.

# CHAPTER 10

F RANCI HAD SPENT days wondering what the Gypsies could be up to. He moved without suspicion among them, for he was one himself, and heard no talk of anything that might be of interest to the inspector. He knew that if De Los Rios heard something, there was something out there to be heard. The inspector rarely sent him out without cause. But, what cause could this be? Buying a pack of cigarettes, he was about to leave the small *tienda* when he heard a heated discussion at a table where three Gypsy men were playing dominos. He paid little attention; these games were always contentious and boisterous.

"We cannot let them do it," one short man shouted. "Why can't they just leave well enough alone?"

"It will take some time to get the permits and have the families agree to all this," added his friend.

"Oh, they will get them all right. Why can't they just leave the dead alone?" the first man continued.

Franci turned his head toward the men, hoping to better listen to their discussion. He lit a cigarette and was now able to more clearly hear what the more vocal of the men was saying.

"The Lorcas will never agree," ranted the first man. "But, I am afraid the government wants this to happen and it might not matter if they agree at all."

"Do you really think they will dig up the graves and find Lorca's body?" the second man questioned.

"Not if the Gypsies have anything to say about it."

The second man continued, "What can they do to stop the government? The whole place will be surrounded by police."

Franci felt his body tighten. Could this be what the inspector was hearing? It did not seem to him like anything *that* important, but it might be worth reporting to the inspector. Maybe the inspector would be satisfied and his task would be completed. He welcomed the thought of returning to the usual routine instead of spending so much of his time doing the inspector's bidding. He decided it was worth a try and that the next day he would go back down to Los Campos #3 to see De Los Rios.

"I know the Gypsies don't like this," scoffed the inspector . . . "Who wants to disturb the dead? But I want to know what they are going to do about it. My men are not hearing anything."

Franci's heart sank. He knew by the tone of that comment that his job was not finished. He then saw the smile on the inspector's face — apparently noticing his discomfort.

De Los Rios thought about *El Pacto de Olvido* — the 'Pact of For-getting.' The law passed after Franco's death, whereby Spaniards would not need to fear retribution for all the atrocities that both sides com-mitted during their bloody civil war. The hair on his neck rose as the anger inside him surfaced. What was this new government trying to do? Their attempts at reconciliation just added fuel to the flames of those who had not forgotten, and had refused to forget. He knew old grudges would resurface and he didn't need this aggravation. Inside, he knew he would be unable to change what he saw happening around him. After all, great monuments had been constructed for the victo-rious Fascists, but none were ever erected for the defeated Republican forces. History had been rewritten to exclude all the sacrifices of the dead, loyalist Republicans. People demanded decent burials and memorials for their family members who occupied the mass graves covering the countryside of Spain—all of whom had been forgotten throughout the reign of Franco.

"Come on Franci, did you think this would be that easy? Don't worry amigo; sooner or later you will hear something. I am sure of it, you always do, Franci."

Franci lit a cigarette and glared at De Los Rios as he slid out the door, back down the stairway into the street—wondering what exactly could the Gypsies do about Lorca.

# CHAPTER 11

FOR THE NEXT several weeks, Carlos combed the university library's newspaper archives, finding hundreds of articles written soon after Lorca's disappearance and death. He spent days with the help of a young librarian named Lola, who took a liking to him right away. She enjoyed the fact that he was researching at one of Spain's and Granada's best libraries and took great pride in her knowledge of the library and its contents.

Lola became his guide, pointing him to all of its archives and catalogs and instructing him in their use. She accompanied Carlos throughout new and old sections of the library, where she showed him hundreds of books and essays not easily found through standard card file searches. These comprised mostly small references by unknown authors commenting on the Lorca disappearance in August of 1936. Carlos was very thankful for Lola, who made his days in the library much more productive. His own efforts to locate items had been time consuming and often fruitless. Lola, in contrast, located several doctoral theses, albums of photographs that had been gifted to the library, and scores of letters and telegrams from some of the principals named in Lorca's disappearance. She insisted that he visit the Lorca Museum and spend more time at the *'Huerta de Lorca,'* the house that his family lived in at the time of his death.

"Only there will you be in Lorca's presence, you will feel him, and it will help you know him better," Lola said emphatically.

Carlos realized Lola had taken on his study with as much zeal as he and she had an uncanny sense of what he should be devoting his time to. Carlos spent most afternoons for the next several weeks under Lola's guidance, selecting what she considered to be the most worthwhile articles to aid him in understanding Lorca and the cast of characters he had come in contact with in his last days.

"Don't waste your time with those books," she often scolded when seeing some of the materials he was reviewing. "There is nothing valuable there you don't already know."

Carlos knew he would be lost without her constant help. Yet despite the library's acclaim in Granada, Carlos could not help but question why everything housed in this grand building seemed so disorganized—except to this remarkable young assistant.

Although the events of Lorca's death and the confusion that surrounded those last few days was never made clear by any author, one central theme always emerged. He had been whisked away and murdered by ignorant, vengeful people who bore personal grudges. Is that what the war was about—personal grudges? Carlos believed there had to be much more to it than that.

Carlos greatly enjoyed roaming Granada and getting a feel for the narrow, cobblestone streets of the old city, lined with small bars and restaurants. And breathing the same air as Lorca had so many years ago always brought him closer to the events of those last days. Lola was right about that. He pictured easily what the city had looked like, with its old, dimly-lit street lamps, and the vintage cars that maneuvered the narrow passageways where people still brought goods from the countryside by mule or horseback. He had immersed himself so deeply in the world of 1936 that he often lost sight of the fact that not everyone shared his passion.

One day, he found himself on a particular mission. He had read much about one of Lorca's favorite places that had always been referred to in his biographies. He headed down a side street looking for this old haunt, the Alameda Café.

It was at this café that a group of young men regularly congregated. They always sat at a corner table, the Rinconcillo, and held court. The young poets, musicians and artists of Lorca's university years gathered here for their daily *tertulia*—round table discussions that touched on politics, poetry, music, and anything they thought worthy of consideration. Lorca's brother Francisco was also among those who attended and appreciated his brother's special talent. Federico had already published *Libros de Poemas,* a book of poems that had appeared in serial format in several magazines in Madrid. Here at the Alameda is where Lorca performed best, in front of an audience of friends. He recited verses and captivated them with his quirky physical motions and eccentric style. Carlos remembered that Lorca was renowned for his lectures and probably invented his narrative style in the presence of these good friends.

After Lorca moved to Madrid, he would always return to the Alameda every summer to renew those friendships. He also came back to Granada every July 18th to be with his family as his father shared with him the same Saint's Day. In Spain, as Carlos well knew, one's Saint's Day—Saint Federico, in this case—was as important as a birthday and was always to be spent with the family.

Lorca also looked forward to seeing the composer Manuel de Falla, who had relocated in Granada to a *carmen*—garden—at the foot of the entrance to the Alhambra. Falla took an immediate liking to Lorca after watching him perform—having heard about him from several of his colleagues at the university. The impetuous, young, self-absorbed poet and the older religious composer spent much time together playing music as Lorca tried out his latest verses with his new friend.

The bartender at the Café Alameda was a jovial, balding man who watched Carlos looking at all the mementos of the Rinconcillo adorning the walls. Carlos sat at the bar and ordered a *vino blanco*—white wine—and asked him if he knew much about the poet Lorca. He smiled and replied that it was a question he was accustomed to since so many people came here inquiring the same about the poet.

"I would appreciate anything you could share with me to help me understand García Lorca. I am writing a book about his life. He was a complicated man with so much controversy surrounding his death. What confuses me most are the circumstances that unfolded during his last few days …"

The bartender interrupted before Carlos could finish his thoughts.

"Well, I can tell you that this bar is still frequented by a nephew of Jose Mora Guarnido, a friend of Lorca's who he met while studying at the University of Granada. He was older than Lorca and was an accomplished poet as well. He was well-known in the literary world in Granada and was a daily participant here at the Rinconcillo. One tale this nephew tells is amusing and might offer insight into Lorca's thinking.

"One afternoon, Lorca arrived home apparently late for dinner. His father sat at the table fuming. It was quite well known that his father was not an admirer of poetry or the inclinations of his son, but preferred the more honorable and better-compensated career of law. When he scolded Federico for his tardiness, Federico jumped up and stated that he refused to be locked up in his house before twilight. The table fell silent. At that point, the kitchen maid entered the dining room and asked the younger Lorca on what type of tortilla he would like to dine. In an instant, Federico's father boomed, 'Give him a tortilla made of twilight!'

"The family looked at the stern face of Don Federico, who remained with a serious look, and then at the poet to see his reaction. In unison, the supper table broke out in laughter, including both father and son, at the absurdity of the statement. Apparently, from then on, an understanding was reached between the two.

"This anecdote was repeated at the Rinconcillo to the delight of all attendees, who perfectly understood the quirky behavior of their comrade."

The bartender now looked across at Carlos, ready to relate another insight into the poet.

"From what the nephew tells me, Lorca was an insecure man who constantly sought acceptance from his companions. He was quite a special man, I have heard, who moved to his own music. Here at the Rinconcillo, he could act out his fantasies and exercise his imagination. He could test his ideas with like minds, not fearing he would be reproached. They were a group way ahead of their time in everything—sharing ideas few *Granadinos* understood.

"It was the ideas that many *Granadinos* resented. This city does not take easily to new ideas or criticism. We are a very conservative bunch here in Granada."

# CHAPTER 12

ARLOS LOVED the architecture of the old city. The Moors'
traditional home was called *carmen* or *karm* in the Arabic. These
were stucco houses enclosed by walls that lined the perimeter.
They were abundant in the *Albayzin* and not necessarily large in
dimension. Inside were lush green vegetable gardens and shade trees
that protected the inhabitants from the hot sun. The occupants passed
leisurely hours in the flower gardens that complemented the fruits and
vegetables they grew. Many had extravagant walkways and fountains
where the sounds of chirping birds and gurgling water could be heard.
It was easy to become accustomed to this half-Spanish, half-Moorish
style of living, which was so different from anything he had experienced
elsewhere. Carlos thought them small Alhambras—self-contained
and self-sufficient. That is why Lorca must have loved Granada so, he
thought. Lorca must have loved the grandeur of the Alhambra, and the
grandeur of the city that surrounded it.

Carlos knew that that the Alhambra was Granada. He also knew
in his heart that Lorca must have thought the same. It was the soul of
the city. Carlos reasoned that it must have been Lorca's motivation to
collect and bring the native music and musicians of the land back to

this Moorish fortress. He *had* to return them to their origins. He knew that symbolically the Alhambra would be the perfect location in which to capture the music Granada was slowly losing.

Carlos had read much about the friendship between one of Spain's greatest composers, Manuel de Falla y Matheu, and Lorca, one of its outstanding poets. He was intrigued how this older composer had recognized early on the young poet's special gifts. The two understood that the traditional folk Andaluz music, the *Cante Jondo*, was inseparable from Granada, and that it had a powerful influence from which the city derived its life and meaning. They agreed on the need to collaborate to rescue it from the commercialism that it was undergoing. The city's identity was built on this strong foundation whose cement was its *Cante Jondo*, the Alhambra and the people of Granada. They were the inseparable ingredients that defined Granada. They feared that this music would be forgotten and relegated to an unworthy position, a position that they were sure it did not represent and could not tolerate. Their collaboration resulted in the *Flamenco* contest. The great Spanish artist Pablo Picasso, then a young man, was called to make the backdrop in the main hall of the *Plaza de los Aljibes* where the singers would perform. This Plaza separates the Alcazaba, or military fortress, from the Alhambra, or great palace. One invited judge to this competition was Andres Segovia, a famed Andaluz classical guitarist. The government and the local businessmen of Granada provided the funding for the event. Cash prizes were awarded to the top ten contestants.

The contest was a success and word of it was published in all the newspapers of Spain. The two top winners were Diego Bermudez, an elderly man of seventy-four who was said to have walked one hundred kilometers to the competition. Second place went to a young boy of twelve years named Manolo Caracol, who was from a renowned Gypsy family of singers and bullfighters. This music was the soul of Granada . . . the soul of the Alhambra . . . and the soul of Lorca. And now, Carlos felt it was becoming part of *his* soul.

How could Lorca ever have expected that his hometown would be where he would meet his end? Despite all the beauty of this wonderful city, Carlos sensed that Granada had a dark side that he was yet to discover.

# CHAPTER 13

ON MANY MORNINGS, Carlos arose in his hotel room at first light. He would always leave early so he could spend time alone in the old palace of the *Nazaris*, the family name of the last Moorish kings of this fortress. In this palace, Washington Irving, the famed American author, spent much of his time writing during 1829. His headless horseman from *The Legend of Sleepy Hollow* is taken from a Moorish tale told to him by the family charged with maintenance of the Alhambra. These were the same chambers that King Phillip V of Spain, together with his wife, Elizabeth of Parma, had restored in Renaissance Italian style in the early eighteenth century. Carlos pictured Irving gloriously passing his days here looking out over the Garden of Generalife and the Albayzin below. What a time that must have been, and he envied the solitary condition that Irving encountered passing his days while writing his famous tales. The great halls of the palace, in this home of kings, are stunning, with Moorish columns and shallow pools, whose cool waters reflect the hues and colors of their surroundings. It was the equal of India's Taj Mahal, Carlos thought — so majestic and inspiring in its shapes and forms.

Carlos thought often of those Moorish kings, but mostly of the saga of its last king, Muhammad the Twelfth, or *Boabdil.* This king was born under auspicious circumstances that the court's astrologers deemed unlucky. He was given the name *Zogoybi*—the unlucky—but was more commonly referred to as *El Chico*—the boy—due to his small stature.

If one were to look for the cause of sadness that hovers over Granada, you would probably have to consider the very first day where it may have all begun. When Fernando and Isabel accepted the surrender of the Kingdom of Granada from Boabdil at the palace of the Alhambra, it was the end of seven hundred years of Moorish rule and the re-conquest of Spain was now complete. The Arabic culture that had transformed Spain was banished from the Iberian Peninsula. It was a joyous day for the Spaniards, as this was the last vestige of the Moors and would effectively end the hundreds of years of conflict between Christian and Moor. Finally, all of Spain would be united under Catholic control. It represented ruination for the Moors, who believed their king to be a coward for acquiescing so easily to the Spaniards' demands without putting up more of a fight. It was the consummation of the prophecy of their unlucky king.

The history of Christian-Moorish wars was centuries long, marked by truces, land concessions on both sides and, in many instances, the joining of forces to defeat a common foe, be it Christian or Moor.

It is true that the Spaniards who demanded this arrangement held Boabdil's son hostage after defeating him in battle. They reasoned that the Moorish king would not risk more war and be rendered basically helpless. Perhaps this was his reason for conceding so easily his beloved city. Many Moors thought poorly of this decision to abandon their beautiful capital without waging an all-out fight.

Upon leaving the red fortress, Boabdil headed for temporary asylum that the Spaniards had arranged for him close to the city Almeria on the southern coast. Exiting the Alhambra, his entourage stopped on a hill so that the defeated king could take a last gaze upon the city he was abandoning. His faithful lieutenants and many Moorish nobles intently watched their forlorn king. Riding at his side, his mother Aisha felt nothing but disgust for her son. She reprimanded him when she saw her son with tears in his eyes. Always his most avid supporter and source of strength, she scolded him, "Do not cry like a woman what you could not defend like a man!"

This hill, *El Suspiro del Moro*—the Last Sigh of Moor—is still a favorite stopping place where people stop and reflect about what the last Moorish king must have seen and thought.

# CHAPTER 14

FEDERICO SAT QUIETLY on the cushioned seat of the train, the Andalusian Express. He had rented a sleeper car for the overnight trip to Granada. His old time friend and confidant, Rafael Martinez Nadal, who was part of the Rinconcillo and with whom he lived when first arriving in Madrid, sent him off. Nadal begged Federico not to leave, fearing for the safety of his poet friend. Federico listened but was adamant that Granada, his home would be safer. As the two friends said goodbye on the platform Federico noticed a man whom he recognized and quickly hugged and kissed his friend saying, "I know that man, he is a lizard. Let me board quickly," and swiftly found the train's sleeper coach and closed the curtains to his private cabin.

Federico insisted on leaving Madrid, knowing his brother and sister would not be able to attend the annual summer retreat with the family at their home in Granada. Mostly, his mother would be terribly disappointed if he were unable to come. Lorca was deep in thought and apprehensive. More than worried, he was deathly afraid. That constant doom that always lingered within him, the fear that gave birth to his creativity, was paralyzing him now. He had always been fearful.

Lorca remembered the day when he first mounted a pony with his brother Francisco. He thought of their family cat that had caught a bird and devoured it in front of him. Even when he visited Salvador Dali's family in Catalonia, at their seaside summer home in Cadaquez, he would never enter the ocean water alone, so frightened he was of harm. Dali's sister, Anna Maria, would always accompany Lorca, holding his hand and both reassuring and consoling him.

He was glad to be returning to his family in Granada, where his doting mother would pamper him. Madrid and Spain were in turmoil at that time, and the political situation became worse with each passing day. Assassinations and robberies were daily occurrences, and the worldwide economic downturn was felt terribly in Spain.

Just a few days before, the Monarchist Calvo Sotelo had been executed by assault squads of the right. The political scene was in shreds. Federico was not and had never been political, although he always sided with the forgotten common man through his music, readings and verse. In fact, he detested politics and the cruelty that man often perpetrated upon his fellow man in its name. Lorca's mission had always been to bring art, music and poetry to the people. He smiled as he remembered the 'La Barraca'—the traveling theater group he founded which was reminiscent of the 16th century Spanish troubadours with their portable stages and plays. It was his way of bringing culture to the people. He had very much enjoyed staging puppet shows with his maids when he was younger and loved the dialogue and comical banter of the characters. The new Republican government had financed these traveling *barracas* in various locations throughout the country, all administered by Lorca. And it was his old friend, Fernando de los Rios, who had supplied the financing for this endeavor through his position in the government.

Now, all that was in the past and the country was headed in a direction he could not understand. An ambitious general named Francisco Franco had declared rebellion and was organizing troops in Africa for a mutiny against the sitting Republican government. Franco knew that conservative Granada would be friendly to his rebellion ... something that Lorca's closest friends thought as well, but which had not even entered his mind.

Lorca was afraid—*terrified*. He stared out the train's window and daydreamed about how the events of his life had unfolded. His melancholy and morose mood had engulfed him like a fine mist. This gloom, his constant partner, descended on and accompanied him, always his doleful companion. At times, it drained him of all his energy, and yet so powerful and invigorating was this gloom inside of him that he would stay awake night after night writing with little or no sleep. It was at times like these he wrote best—when this intoxicating sadness crept up from his heart, through his arm and out of his pen. It was an Andaluz sadness—his own sadness. Looking out the train's window he reflected on earlier, happier times.

He reminisced about those years in Granada at the Alameda restaurant—the glorious times he spent at the Rinconcillo, at the corner table. His ability to describe details in his own inimitable fashion brought roars of laughter to all. Lorca was a natural born storyteller who grew up with verse and music, and his odd countenance and dress, his brusque clumsy movements and uncertain manner captivated these close friends.

He had shown no interest in attending university, though he managed to please his father by barely getting a degree in law with the aid of close friends who tutored him and cajoled him onward. They understood the pressure he put on himself. He recalled his university professor and friend, Fernando de los Rios, the same man who funded his La Barraca and recognized his young student's raw talent. It was he who convinced his father that bigger and better things awaited him in the capital Madrid. There was an intellectual movement budding there that he knew Lorca must become part of.

Once Federico arrived in Madrid, he lived in the 'Residencia de Estudiantes,' the student residence that was similar to his Rinconcillo in atmosphere but with the great city of Madrid as its tutor and backdrop. The people he met changed his life: Juan Ramon Jimenez, the poet; Luis Buñuel, the cinematographer; Dali, the avant-garde painter; and many others. In Madrid, he flourished. Federico lit a cigarette, thinking of those carefree days when life was without complexity.

He remembered the grand piano at the Residencia and smiled, thinking of all the good times he enjoyed there. During those wonderful years, spanning 1918 to 1928, he was king of his court, singing all the Andaluz folk songs in his deep and raspy voice, to the delight of his housemates. He recited his poetry to eager listeners. Several publishers invited him to contribute his verse to their magazines. And he was invited to recite before groups, and numerous publications enthusiastically included him in their pages. His fame quickly spread though the literary circles of Madrid.

Lorca next thought back on his trip with de los Rios to New York, where he was overwhelmed by the great city. Traveling across the ocean, he doubted his reasons for going. He spent long hours staring contemplatively at the sea. Along the way, he made friends with a small boy who was going to meet his father in New York. When they landed, both he and the boy hugged, crying in each other's arms. He recalled how lonely he was to be in a city where communicating was so difficult. He laughed at himself about how unable he was to speak English and how he ordered the same food daily, ham and eggs, for want of more words and his embarrassment at asking for anything different. He recalled his dormitory room at Columbia University and his feeble attempts to learn his host country's language, despite being enrolled for weeks in an English course.

He loved the parties and nightlife of this awesome city that seemed so mechanized and impersonal. To him, America was largely free of social mores and rules of public behavior. He thought of this American religion as cold and detached. In his mind, it did not compare to the rituals and rites of the Catholic Church. However, the tall skyscrapers and lights of the city mesmerized him. Times Square was "higher than the moon." He smiled, thinking of all the letters he had written his parents describing his perceptions of the great city and how much he was enjoying himself. He did not dare tell them how lonely and isolated he felt.

His most favorite destination was Harlem. How he loved to sit in the jazz clubs and listen to that new American sound. He saw the black neighborhoods with the tremendous bigotry that existed in New York, the same as the bigotry the Gypsies suffered in Granada. Yet both peoples were able to reach inside themselves and produce an original music that was born in their souls. Their roots of pain and isolation he recognized immediately as coming from their forgotten place in time. He compared the *Cante Jondo* to the Negro Jazz. Their music was the only escape from a world of suffering and despair.

It was New York that inspired him to work again. His head filled up quickly with new verses—verses that were taking a dramatically different form. These new poems were less descriptive, less understandable, and much more abstract. He loved to read Walt Whitman, whose love of America with its egalitarian notions and themes of love he found so profoundly moving. He loved Whitman's style, free of conventions, and he knew that this was a form that suited him well also. It was a form that depended on illusions—a form he would adopt in all his subsequent verse and plays.

Lorca laughed out loud when he recalled his attempt at writing a movie script with a Mexican acquaintance he had made in New York. He thought much of his friend, Luis Buñuel, the moviemaker he had shared quarters with in Madrid's Residencia. I too could make films, Lorca thought. However, he later abandoned that project, preferring the give-and-take between actors and audience in live theater productions. The poetry he created in New York resulted directly from the sharp images the city impressed on him. The result was a catalog of poems he intended combining into one collection. They were sometimes grim descriptions—a collection of the emotions of life and people in the great city. *Poeta in Nueva York* became an international hit, reaffirming his place as one of the new, exciting poets of his time.

Lorca had even witnessed a man's body prostrate on the street resulting from a leap from one tall building. This vision, more than any other, reinforced his whole concept of America as devoid of real meaning and without genuine values—a nation controlled by the few and interested only in monetary gains. America was so complicated, and he longed more and more for Spain with its greater simplicity.

He lit another cigarette while watching the barren countryside pass him by. He was both relieved and glad. He thought of Granada, the wonderful Alhambra. He would be glad to see all his friends. He looked forward to visiting one of his mentors, the composer Manuel de Falla, where he would spend long hours conversing with his old friend and colleague. He thought of his work, the *Romancero de los Gitanos*—*Gypsy Ballads*—which had been acclaimed throughout the artistic world. Falla deserved much credit for this work, since he had been so instrumental in their festival of *Cante Jondo* at the Alhambra. Federico resented being branded as the 'Gypsy poet,' but also understood that it was this work which brought him his fame and notoriety.

He reflected about how all his plays had been received in Madrid and Paris, and later in New York and South America. He was happy with his two latest accomplishments, the tragedy *The House de Bernardo Alba,* and *Thus Let Five Years Pass.* And he thought about everything he had done and everything that still remained for him to accomplish.

Lorca was eager to travel to Mexico—he would land in New York and then take a glorious weeklong train ride to Mexico, seeing new sights all along the way. He had met a marvelous young Mexican woman in New York, Antonieta Rivas Mercado, with whom he had made plans to join in Mexico to cooperate in joint theatre ventures. However, to his great disappointment, that plan was soon abandoned when the superb Mexican artist tragically died in Paris. Despite this, his enthusiasm for Mexico was not diminished.

But here he sat, frozen with fear. He wondered if the man he had noticed while boarding the train, the one he recognized and detested, was following him to his home. Lorca exhaled heavily, lighting

yet another cigarette. Everything would work out; after all, he was going home. He tried to relax. He reassured himself by remembering that
his family was prosperous and had enjoyed much stature in Granada.
He was sure he would be safe there. He repeated this mantra over and
over; he was sure it would keep him safe. He lowered the train's window on that hot July night, closed his eyes, and disappeared into a fret-
ful and restless sleep.

# CHAPTER 15

**D**ON CARLOS, *un momento ... por favor* ... one minute, please. Someone has left you a note here at the reception," shouted Manolo, seeing Carlos hurrying through the hotel lobby toward the stairway.

Carlos' last few afternoons had been spent at the Lorca Museum in Fuente Vaqueros, Lorca's birthplace, and at his family summer home at the *Huerta de Don Vincente*. It was eerie to see the bedroom where Lorca had spent so much time. Carlos could imagine Lorca putting his feet on the floor and stretching to begin another day. The house remained exactly as it had been since 1936. Walking on the earthenware-tiled floors, Carlos felt the Lorca family presence throughout the small house, with pictures of the family in every room. The piano at which Federico had sat for hours was set in a corner of the small salon and hadn't moved since last it was played by the poet. Federico spent many happy hours entertaining his friends and family.

As Carlos moved throughout the entire house, he sensed Lorca's desperation in those final days of August 1936. The house was alive and gave Carlos a queasy feeling. Carlos felt subdued and depressed as this intimate relationship with the poet was forming inside him. He could feel the anxiety that Lorca suffered, and it made him uneasy. He left the house and took a deep breath. Outside, he instantly felt more relaxed as the Lorca home loosened its grip on him. With each new revelation about the poet came a tremendous satisfaction and at the same time a fear he could not explain. Something was drawing him closer to a place he hardly understood. He became so absorbed with Lorca that at times he was unaware of anything else of importance. The feeling that some force was guiding him, directing him to retrace the footsteps of Lorca overwhelmed him. He was unsure why he should feel so ill at ease about something that occurred so long ago. Carlos looked forward to discussing these feelings with Lola, who was always excited to see him enter the library. She sensed his devotion and continued enthusiasm for his project. Lola lifted his spirits — especially on days when he thought the whole project absurd. She had seen many people delve so completely into their topics that they seemed to lose themselves for a time. Lola assured Carlos that he should continue and that it was all right to feel the way he did.

He started to doubt whether a novel was even appropriate for such a revered and great person. Was there anything he could really add about the life of someone who had been the topic of so much discussion?

Carlos took the note that Manolo handed him and was delighted to see it was from Nadya, advising that the following Sunday evening, the long awaited reunion he looked so forward to would convene. He anticipated that the *Cante Jondo*, described to him by Neftali, would be a true highlight of his stay. It was Thursday, and he had planned to spend the next several days in the library, digging ever deeper into the identities and backgrounds of the shadowy characters who were involved in Lorca's demise.

Lola had confided to him that there was a special section of the library where entrance might be gained to references referring to this chaotic period of Lorca's confinement prior to his execution. As a rule, it was reserved for the university's professors, but she had received permission to allow Carlos access to this section. Among the documents it contained were bound books of letters and correspondence written by many of those thought to have played a part in Lorca's final days. Relatives of those involved—now deceased themselves—had also submitted many of the letters. Lola emphasized the importance of their content to Carlos who understood these were the primary source materials he had been seeking. There had been much conjecture as to the causes and motivations of those individuals involved in Lorca's murder, even as little had been substantiated. Carlos spent hours deciphering the letters' penmanship and sorting them according to their importance. Many were from one person who continually denied any wrongdoing in the whole affair. He was a low-level Falange official named Alonso.

Carlos had known that Lorca had been abducted by a typographer named Ramon Ruiz Alonso while staying at the house of Luis Rosales, a noted *Granadino* poet and a founder of the Granada Falange. The Rosales family was friendly with the Lorcas. Ruiz Alonso published a daily for the Accion Catolica, a Falangist action organization. Carlos was told that Ruiz Alonso was still alive; however, the possibility of meeting him was at best remote. Although Lola said that it would be difficult to arrange such a meeting, her enthusiasm that it might occur was lacking. Ruiz Alonso was now old and had conducted scores of interviews, never revealing—in fact, always denying—that he shared any fault for the Lorca murder. Lola instead supplied him with a list of names of other prominent *Granadino* citizens, mostly all older now, who she believed might be of some assistance. She remained quite adamant in her sentiment that they would probably not agree to discuss anything at all. Apparently, the Lorca family wanted to put all this behind them, as did most of the rest of the citizens of Granada.

Opening new doors was sure to open new wounds and hard feelings. The Civil War was barely forty years old and many survivors from both sides were alive and still harbored deep grudges. Many still felt tremendous animosity about the war and hoped for an opportunity to settle scores according to the diminutive librarian.

# CHAPTER 16

S UNDAY ARRIVED QUICKLY. The day was overcast and the
heat and mugginess that clung close to the ground were signs
of yet another oppressively hot day. In the city, there was a
foreboding clamor. It was holy day and the usual concerto of church
bells resonated throughout the city like instruments in a symphony.
Each bell seemed to be eagerly anticipating its turn to sound.

Carlos walked down *Cuesta de los Gomerez* anticipating an evening
of pure delight, but more than that, he was excited at the prospect of
another chance to cast his gaze on the beautiful Gypsy girl. For days
he realized that something special had come over him. His thoughts
kept returning to visions of the evening they had spent together. Despite his best intentions to concentrate on work, he often found himself caught up in daydreams of the entrancing beauty of this woman he
hardly knew—the tantalizing way she danced, and the face and smile
that melted him. He repeatedly relived the moments of that evening
when she had invited him to share in the family's dinner. He thought
about how gracefully she glided with her tall, comely figure, accented
by a dark, lustrous complexion.

Carlos had experienced his share of romances and well knew
the sensation he felt when he was attracted to a woman. But Nadya

was different. She left him unusually off-balance and unable to think clearly. He thought only of wanting to see her again. Nadya had become an unanticipated distraction as she occupied more and more of his thoughts. She was nudging up next to Lorca in importance, and that gave Carlos a confused sense of priority.

Arriving at the *Plaza Nueva,* Carlos noticed that most of the tables in the square were full of people enjoying the evening's cooler air; shoeshine boys were passing among the tables looking for prospective customers; lottery vendors waved their tickets barking tomorrow's lucky numbers; and busy waiters were rushing about, carrying trays overflowing with *tapas* and wine to tables crowded with laughing patrons. He bypassed the plaza and turned right at the old stone church to scale the *Paseo de Los Tristes* as the busy traffic, consisting mostly of taxis and motorbikes, passed him by. He suddenly felt himself becoming anxious. Anticipating another meeting with Nadya gave him a queasy feeling. He felt absurd as this unfamiliar feeling washed over him, but more than anything, he wanted the evening to go smoothly. Arriving at the cave's entrance, he paused, looking up at the Alhambra.

Wish me luck, he thought to himself, as a flock of blackbirds passed overhead.

The street was clear and several people were gathered at the doorway. As Carlos stepped through the entrance, a young Gypsy man approached and wished him good evening. Unlike during his previous visit, there were only a few people talking in small groups. He had anticipated a much greater attendance. The cave appeared much larger than he remembered, but otherwise was the essentially the same, with chairs clinging to their positions next to the rounded walls and dim lamps. Three men were at one side of the room, deep in conversation, and they took pause when they noticed Carlos' entrance.

"Carlos, *bienvenido,* welcome," a voice called out from behind.

He turned to see Nadya moving toward him with a gleaming smile, wearing a plain black sleeveless dress that rested slightly above her knees. Her shoulder-length black hair was wavy and pleasingly unruly. Adorning her ears were thin, silver rings that glistened in the evening light. She wore no makeup and to Carlos, it seemed that she had the kind of intoxicating natural beauty from which any addition could only detract. She wore leather thong sandals that revealed delicately slender feet and toes whose scarlet hued nails matched those on her fingers. She brushed her cheeks against his in a typical Spanish welcome.

Carlos consciously held his breath as Nadya took him by the arm and led him toward a row of seats.

"Please come sit by me, Carlos," she requested, while moving her body closer to his.

Carlos' heart was pounding so hard he was sure she could hear it. He could not remember being so undone by a woman's presence.

They sat at one corner of the room where the three men were discussing something, occasionally raising their voices—unaware of anyone around them.

"What a special evening we have," Nadya enthusiastically announced. "We have a nephew of Diego Bermudez, one of the winning performers of the great *Cante Jondo* Festival held at the Alhambra. He is a close friend of my father."

"The very same Diego Bermudez that attended the concurso, presented by Manuel de Falla and García Lorca?" Carlos questioned.

"Yes, though he himself will be the first to tell you that we will never hear that type of talent again. Those were different times; people sang all the time, not just to perform as now."

The three men seated next to them were now engaged in a heated exchange and their voices were growing steadily louder. One of the older men, surely a Gypsy, said "This is not something that we should be doing, something will go wrong, mark my words."

Nadya glanced at them nervously as if she were embarrassed by the content of their conversation. She glanced at Carlos with a half-smile and noticed the quizzical look on his face.

"Don't concern yourself with them, they always argue," she said dismissively. Just then, an older man came out from behind the curtain and made his way to a chair where the *Flamenco* dancers had been seated the previous evening. He had a frail appearance, was slight of build, and his gray hair and a weather-worn face made him look as if he were always tired. His clothes were tattered and shabby, suggesting his humble origins. Just then, the three loud Gypsies noticed the arrival of the old man and suspended their argument, looked around and found several seats together. Carlos noticed that several other people had entered and were being seated, among them Neftali. He approached the old man and greeted him warmly, kissing him on both cheeks and assisting him to his seat. The elderly reciprocated with kisses and hugs as Neftali introduced him to the fifteen or so people who were already seated. The cave's doors were then shut. This was a special occasion, Carlos thought. Some of those seated greeted the man, who exchanged pleasantries with people he obviously knew.

Neftali then exchanged looks with the old man and started to clap his hands slowly and deliberately. In a deep, husky voice, the old man began with eyes closed, to sing in the traditional Anduluz,

> *"Aonde me llevas?" (Where are you taking me?)*
> *"Que no te pueo seguir;" (Where I cannot follow you;)*
> *"No me metes en camino" (Do not put me on a path)*
> *"Que yo no puea salir." (Where I cannot leave.)*

The old man's voice quivered as he delivered the lyrics of song after sad song. Everyone's eyes focused on this man who connected his song to the people riveted to their seats.

Nadya's eyes were welling up with tears. He was telling his own story. He was telling *her* story. He was telling a story that everyone in the room knew. It was the Gypsy story. The expressions on everyone's faces showed that he had exposed their inner feelings; he had touched a place that belonged only to them. They were Gypsies and this was their music. It was beyond Carlos' understanding how the life stories and pain of generations could be caught in the solitary voice of a singer such as this. The man continued to sing for more than an hour, stopping occasionally to drink a glass of water a young man kept refilling.

To Carlos' surprise, Neftali joined in as the two men took turns reciting the forlorn lyrics, their throats vibrating with these traditional songs of alienation. Close to midnight, both men exhaustingly hung their heads down—bringing to conclusion this magical moment. They had spent their emotions and the assembled audience seemed as drained as the old man and Neftali. There was a long silence and little applause. Mostly they gave their approval by shouting their appreciation. Nadya then reached over and took Carlos's hand, "I am happy that we could share this with you. You are very special, Carlos—my father enjoys speaking with you."

She then stood up to assist two young men who were beginning to serve refreshments of beer and cheese with hot bread. The three men who were so engaged in their heated discussion left together after shaking hands with the two singers they obviously were well-acquainted with. Nadya approached Carlos and took his hand, walking him to the cave's exit. Neftali turned his head toward the couple, watching their exit toward the doorway. He called out to Nadya to stop.

"I would like to introduce Carlos to my friend."

As Carlos and Neftali approached him, a broad smile broke across the aged man's face. He moved to take the hands of the approaching couple. The old singer wrapped his hands graciously around Carlos' and thanked him for permitting him to sing.

Neftali looked at Carlos, "Promise me Carlos that you will return here often to join us."

"I enjoy your company and thank you very much for coming. It also appears that my daughter enjoys your company as well if you don't mind me telling you."

Nadya's face blushed as her father gave Carlos an approving smile.

"I mean to come again, hopefully quite often, thank you."

The street was muggy, but a slight breeze was a welcome relief from the stuffy heat of the cave. Nadya stood beside Carlos with small beads of sweat on her cheeks. People were moving up and down the street laughing, lovers holding hands, and families wheeling baby carriages on their way home. The crowds at this late hour were normal for Granada.

Soon the couple remained alone on the sidewalk underneath the gaze of the Alhambra. Carlos gathered up his nerve.

"May I escort you to your home? I would love to see the *Sacromonte* with someone who knows it so well."

She smiled and nodded her head while gazing at him with those dark eyes that intrigued him so.

As they walked up the *Carrera del Rio Darro*, he told her of his days spent in the library and his progress with Lorca. She listened and agreed that it was an interesting effort and inquired how long his stay would be in Granada.

"Until I feel comfortable with the facts ... mostly why there is so much confusion about why he was killed." Nadya nodded and smiled as always as they climbed the hills toward her home.

Within what seemed like a few minutes they arrived at *Calle Zafra,* a short, narrow street of three blocks and then turned right on *Calle de los Reyes,* which appeared to Carlos to be one of the larger avenues of the Albayzin. No one was on the street and the old fashioned street lamps, *faroles,* gave this district an identity all its own. The neighborhood was trapped in time, lending it an appearance of the last century. To Carlos, it felt as if he were passing through a time that had been all but forgotten. Change was slow to arrive here—unlike the hubbub of the more modern central city below. The streets were lined with small houses no more than two stories in height—most with gardens and small fences.

"The city does not reach out to the Gypsy community and help us as it should," Nadya remarked, probably reading Carlos' mind. "Probably it is for the best."

Carlos reached over and took Nadya's hand, and she wrapped her fingers around his. As they walked, they breathed in the various smells from the homes preparing to serve late night dinners. The lights shining at the Alhambra, visible in the distance, made Carlos feel how lucky these people were to always have that fortress so close by.

"I wonder if the Alhambra is watching out for this beautiful Gypsy," Carlos thought.

Soon, a lovely sound filled the air and Carlos' ears strained to identify where it was coming from. It was unmistakable. The slow, beautiful tune captured and saturated the heavy night air. As each soft note floated through the night, he recognized as a sonata by Chopin. Nadya smiled, noticing his surprise.

"Do you like it?" she asked.

"I certainly did not expect to hear the music of Chopin up here in the Gypsy quarter. It is wonderful but seems a bit out of place."

"I am glad you like it. The homes on this street have become accustomed to it at this late hour. It is our after-hours serenade."

As they walked further down the narrow street, the piano's notes increased in volume and clarity, when suddenly, Nadya stopped.

"This is my home."

Carlos looked awkwardly at Nadya and she laughed when she saw the silly look on his face.

The music was clear and crisp as it poured out the open windows into the cobblestone street.

"That is my grandfather playing; he loves to play classical music, especially late at night when he has trouble sleeping."

Carlos was speechless but managed to stammer out, "It is incredible. I mean, he must be an incredible person. May I meet him sometime? His playing is beautiful."

"I am sure you will; thank you for walking me home, Don Carlos."

As she stood on her tiptoes and leaned in, kissing him on the cheek, Nadya whispered, "*Buenas noches*, Carlos."

Turning around and starting down the narrow street, Carlos continued to consume the piano's soft notes that trailed him down the narrow alleyway until they evaporated into the heavy night air. He made his way back down the Albayzin and up the *Cuesta de los Gomerez* toward his hotel, hoping all the while that time might stop for him here in Granada.

# CHAPTER 17

CARLOS SAT IN THE PLAZA NUEVA drinking his usual *cafe con leche* and reading a copy of the *International Herald Tribune*. He glanced at the headlines that hardly held his attention. He noticed how disinterested he was in the events of the world. His whole world at the moment revolved around the library and his new fascination with Nadya. Everything else seemed trivial.

It had been several weeks since he began to reread all the essays, lectures and poetry that Lorca had written. The tragic plays, *Boda de Sangre* (Blood Wedding) and *Yerma,* were the two works that most caught his interest. Lorca had connected to the hopelessness of the peasant *campesino* and the condition of rural, traditional Spanish society. He touched on themes like the plight of women in Spain's male-dominated society that few writers dared to approach. Lorca challenged the unbending and dogmatic role of the church and faith and framed his criticism in his plays. Despite his love for the church's ritual, as Lorca was a brought up a Catholic, his artistic view of Spain's condition was revolutionary and disturbing.

His plays were performed in Madrid, in South America and Europe near the end of his life. These were ominous times in Spain as the political and cultural situation was tugging in two distinct directions, one of change and expression and the other of repression and the status quo.

Democratic ideas and institutions were alien to Spain's thinking as a monarch or strongmen had always ruled there. Carlos thought how daring Lorca was in that toxic atmosphere to present such plays, which questioned the fundamental values of Spain. Many of the church and wealthy classes saw his works as heresy, and viewed even the idea of parliamentary government as a threat.

Carlos found it strange that the church had sided with the fascists throughout the civil war and he had found many pictures in the libraries of Catholic priests giving fascist salutes. Spain was entirely a Catholic country and this had been the case since the expulsion of the Moors and Jews in the fifteenth century. The democratically elected Republican government adopted a more progressive agenda, and enacted many new laws to attempt to break the strangle hold of the rich and of the church. Ultimately, all these changes were to no avail.

Carlos looked up from his paper toward the *Paseo de los Tristes* and watched the people descending from the Albayzin. Many had umbrellas to protect them from the hot afternoon sun. He thought he caught a glimpse of a familiar face coming toward him and stared through the hazy day more intently at the approaching figure. It was a slender young lady moving quickly with a determined look—the same beautiful face he had gazed on the evening before. What he actually saw was not the cheerful face that he knew, but rather one that seemed filled with worry. He rose quickly from his table, and motioned in attempt to catch her attention. Nadya, who was moving rapidly through the crowd, turned in surprised toward him and moved across the plaza in his direction, trying her best to cover the expression she thought he may have noticed.

"*Hola,* Carlos, *que tal,* how are you? What a surprise to see you."

"And I, you. I enjoy sitting in this plaza, watching the people and what luck I must have seeing you again so soon! I was just reading the paper; I haven't been paying much attention to the news lately. Nadya, is something wrong?"

"And is there any good news to be had?" Nadya asked in a half smile.

"You seem worried, is everything ok?"

She looked away, then turned toward Carlos and asked, "Would you like to walk with me?"

Of course he would—he could think of nothing better, he thought to himself, intrigued by her dark eyes, shapely mouth and glistening skin. He hurriedly folded the newspaper and took some *peseta* notes from his pocket, setting them on the table as he motioned to the *camarero* where he had paid.

They walked toward the *Avenida Reyes Catolicos* toward the *Gran Via*, the largest and busiest street in downtown Granada. People scurried down the busy avenue as motorcycles zipped by and horns blared. Carlos looked at Nadya and was pleased to notice her earlier worried look had dissipated, replaced by her usual, radiant visage.

"Is something bothering you, Nadya?" he whispered to her a second time.

Nadya remained silent, though it was apparent something was disturbing her as they walked among the crowds on the *Gran Via*. They soon reached the monument of Isabela La Catolica with Christopher Columbus, a beautiful stone fountain with colored beams of water shooting up in all directions. In it, Columbus is kneeling before Queen Isabela, the bronze figures depicting the queen's capitulations to Columbus' request for his first voyage to the Americas. Carlos remembered that it was here in Granada that the famous queen and explorer had finally sealed the fate of the Americas. Carlos and Nadya turned onto the *Gran Via*, proceeding along the wide avenue with little conversation. Nadya seemed deep in thought. Carlos walked quietly by her side, choosing not to ask her any further questions. At *Calle Marques de Falces* they turned left, near the *Gran Catedral* of Granada, into the original narrow streets of ancient Granada.

They passed a mime dressed in an outfit painted with effervescent gold sprinkles, who stood motionlessly while people tossed a few *centimos* in his hat that lay by his feet. Flies buzzed around his face glistening with sweat and gold, yet not a muscle moved as he held his position.

The nearby cathedral is a tremendous monument of cut stone and stained glass erected upon the major Muslim mosque of the pre-conquest. It was built in 1518 after the defeat of the Boabdil and the Nasrid Empire of Granada. It is the most sacred spot in Granada, visited by multitudes of tourists and revered by the citizens of this Catholic city. Carlos had read that it took some one hundred eighty years for completion. Many of Spain's churches were projects that spanned centuries and were testaments to their religious devotion. Guides circle the *Catedral* and scurry hurriedly among all the passersby, speaking a variety of languages while looking for tourists eager to learn the history of this holy place of worship.

The couple walked a hundred meters down *Los Falces,* behind the Cathedral, where most of the University of Granada is located. These small *callejones,* or narrow streets, hardly allow even a small vehicle to pass. Pedestrians routinely duck into doorways accustomed to this inconvenience. These neighborhoods contain many small plazuelas, small parks where the local inhabitants gather. People come here to sit on the wood benches, read their newspapers or frequent the small cafés and bars that surround them. The plazuelas are commonplace in all Spanish cities. Nadya chose to sit at a small café with only a few outside tables next to a busy newspaper stand where men were buying the daily en route to their homes for lunch. The small park was abuzz with people sitting on benches, taking a few moments to enjoy the birds chirping, and nannies watching their children run and play.

Carlos was thinking of what he might say to Nadya when she suddenly turned toward him and unexpectedly said, "They want to dig up the poet's bones."

Carlos thought and tried to comprehend what had just been said and repeated, "The poet's bones?"

"Yes, they are going to go soon and retrieve his bones before anyone else can."

Carlos looked intently at Nadya. Her hands were folded in her lap and her head was down. She looked relieved that she had shared this burden with someone, and let out a deep sigh. Carlos reached across the table and gently took her chin in his hands, their eyes meeting.

"What poet?" Carlos asked.

"Of course you must know ... the poet Lorca!"

Carlos sat for a moment, dazed, thinking about all his work and all that he knew about the *Granadino* poet—a poet with whom he was so deeply involved and who seemed always nearby in his thoughts. Lorca, to him, was someone to study—one that you could write about and review, but distant enough in an academic sense. He found himself without words, and with the incomprehensible idea that Lorca could ever touch him personally. Certainly, Carlos believed that no one could appreciate more than he Lorca's poetry and genius and have such an immense understanding of his life and his work. After all, wasn't this the reason why he was here—to try and reach out and touch him? Carlos had never really expected to approach Lorca like this, with Nadya so suddenly revealing to him something so unfathomable he never thought or imagined possible. They wanted to steal Lorca's bones and he might know the people that wanted to do it? His response was simple and shallow: "Why do they want Lorca's bones?"

"I don't know ... I just overheard several men talking the other night when we were at the cave. The same men you saw discussing in the corner. They are all friends of my father, all Gypsies. They seemed nervous and angry and papa spent a long time talking to them before you came. When I asked papa he told me that it was all of no account. But, I know of my father's love of Lorca and know he is involved somehow in this. I am worried and afraid for him. Everything just seems so absurd."

Carlos searched his memory about all that occurred the night of the *Cante Jondo*. Yes, he had seen the anxiety of the Gypsy men secreting themselves and deep in discussion. Certainly he knew a lot about Lorca's history, his political leanings, the Civil War and the deep divisions that existed between the left and the right. He knew that the Republican left had never been satisfied ... that they were never able to account for their dead and missing. Of course, the most famous of the unaccountable was the poet Lorca ... buried in one of the many unmarked graves of that period.

Carlos knew that the supposed site of the poet's execution, along with several other men, was in a small town nearby Granada called Viznar. But with this, what could these men possibly be thinking? What could be gained by stealing the bones of the famous poet, buried without a marker almost forty years ago?

All these questions seemed to blur in Carlos' mind as he looked with concern on the worried face of Nadya. He signaled the waiter to bring him the bill, continuing to focus an anxious gaze on Nadya. He stood up, quickly taking her by the hand. She looked up at him timidly and stood up beside him.

"*Vamos,* Nadya. Let's go." Together they headed back toward the Albayzin with Carlos' arm around her waist and her head tilted on his shoulder.

# CHAPTER 18

FRANCI HEREDIA sat at the table smoking, wiping the sweat from his neck in the *Plaza Nueva*. When would this heat let up, he wondered. Granada was always hot in the summer, but this year it was unrelenting. Each day, the thermometer climbed to near forty degrees centigrade and the only respite from the heat was the shade and the umbrellas at these small cafés offering temporary refuge from the glaring sun.

Franci sat at a corner table and ordered black coffee with a glass of ice on the side. He added sugar liberally and poured the steaming coffee over the ice, stirring the contents by sliding the glass back and forth on the metal table. People would stop for a few moments at a time at the water fountain in the middle of the plaza to splash cool water on their faces. It had been several weeks since Franci had seen De Los Rios and he was at a dead end when rumors about the poet once again reached his ears. Maybe it was just due to the government's attempts at identifying the bodies in the mass graves. Granada was abuzz with the daily reports in the papers about the gravesites and the government's insistence in opening them up to identify their occupants.

Franci knew he needed to find a way of uncovering what was going on if something was really happening. De Los Rios would begin to make his life miserable if he did not deliver something soon.

He remembered one friend, José, a Gypsy taxi driver who operated from his station here in the *Plaza Nueva*. José was always a reliable source of good information — a contact who seemed to know and feel the heartbeat of the city. Franci had stopped by the line of waiting taxis inquiring for José, knowing that he would show sooner or later. He lit another cigarette, anticipating his arrival. Twenty or so minutes passed and Franci recognized José pulling in to take his place in the back of the queue of waiting cabs. As was the cabbie's custom, he stepped out, leaving the car in neutral, and rolled it several feet forward — placing his hand on its steering wheel through the open driver's side window. He then glanced up and saw Franci, throwing him a grin of recognition while leaning inside the window to make sure the brake was set. José was a tall, heavy-set Gypsy with the same olive skin and curly black hair that marked their identity. He huffed and puffed from this small exertion. Just then, another driver hollered something and pointed toward Franci's table. José nodded his head and strode across the *Plaza Nueva*, arriving at Franci's side. Without asking, he pulled out a metal chair and sat down, puffing heavily — despite the short distance he had just traveled. Franci raised his hand for the waiter and ordered a Coca Cola, which was quickly brought back with a glass of ice.

"Juan said you wanted to see me, so here I am. *Que pasa*, what's happening?" the driver inquired.

"You hear well. How are you? The family? *Todo bien?* ... Everybody good?"

"*Si, Señor* ... What can I do for my friend Franci?"

"I know that you know the countryside like the back of your hand. You travel to all the small towns around Granada ... I was wondering if you have been to Viznar lately."

"Certainly, I go there often — it's a tourist destination and lately it seems that everyone is interested in that town … what with all the talk of Lorca and the government's interest in exhuming the gravesites."

"What types of passengers go there, José?" Franci leaned closer to the rotund driver concentrating on his response.

"Mostly tourists, like I said for it is on the route of Lorca. I take people first to his old hometown of Fuente Vaqueros, then to the Museum, and then to the *Huerta*, where his family used to pass their summers and sometimes, for the more interested parties, to Viznar, where they say he was executed."

"Just tourists, then?" pressed Franci, as the big taxi driver looked at him more intently and took another cigarette from his pack. José paused for a moment and then continued slowly, "Lately, there have been a lot of our people visiting the Viznar site as well—probably because of all the renewed interest. They always stay outside the cordoned off area trying to get a view of the death site."

"Why are they visiting? Do you know? … Just to pay their respects to our Gypsy poet?"

"No idea why, but I can tell you there is a small group that has been there several times in the last few weeks."

"Who are they? … Are they from here?"

"You probably know them all. They are Gypsies who work in the tourist caves. Isn't that where you spend most of your time, Franci?"

José's words fell on deaf ears, as Franci was deep in thought, his mind floating away to the caves, drawing mental images of all his friends and family that worked in *Flamenco*. He stood up abruptly, throwing some pesetas for the two drinks on the table and leaving without even a goodbye. The taxi driver seemed unfazed as he stood up, taking a last gulp of his soda and shouting, *"Adios, amigo."*

# CHAPTER 19

C ARLOS AWOKE as the first rays of the morning sun shone through the window of his hotel. He opened the sliding door and sat down on the small balcony's edge overlooking the city of Granada below. He was looking forward to today, having accepted an invitation to Nadya's house for dinner this evening, but he felt a bit jittery as well. His work on Lorca was proceeding at a slower pace than he had wished but now, with the revelation Nadya had shared with him, everything had come to a complete halt. He was confused. He could not possibly imagine what anyone might want with Lorca's bones. His thoughts jumped from the worried face of Nadya to the three men he had seen in the cave. Looking out over the city, he felt apprehensive but hopeful the evening would pass without incident.

Carlos' relationship with Nadya, on the other hand, was going well. When they were together, he was happy. In the past several weeks they had seen each other many times; taking long walks through the streets of Granada; frequenting many of the coffee and pastry shops they both adored; or just sitting in a park—laughing and tossing nuts to the pigeons. She had not mentioned any more about her father or Lorca, and Carlos decided it was best not to bring up the subject again.

The concern Nadya had shown for her father seemed forgotten. Although Carlos did not dare to discuss it, the matter remained in the back of his mind. Several times he wanted to raise the topic but always reconsidered so as to not upset Nadya again—at least not yet. His interest in Lorca would not let his mind drift from the day she had confided in him her fears. Tonight he would see Neftali and try to get a feeling for this whole affair. He dressed quickly and left his room, walking up the hill from the Alixares Hotel toward the cemetery. He walked quickly in the bright morning's sun, trying to make some sense of the situation. It was clear to him that he needed to talk of Lorca with Neftali without upsetting Nadya.

Carlos returned to his room, and after a quick shower and shave, headed down the stairs to the lobby of the Alixares. The lobby was a mass of tourists—mostly Japanese—who were assembling around a tour guide who spoke both Spanish and Japanese. They were off to their appointment at the Alhambra. While this was going on, Manolo was shouting instructions from behind the reception desk to several of the bellmen. He urged the staff to move the crowd along quickly to make way for a loud group of students who were arriving simultaneously. Carlos moved toward the far side of the lobby where Pepe the waiter greeted him. Carlos ordered his usual *cafe con leche* and the traditional *Granadino* breakfast of toast with olive oil and tomato. Reaching over to grab a copy of the morning newspaper lying on the countertop nearby, Carlos skipped through the pages until a small headline caught his eye:

THE SOCIALIST GOVERNMENT AGREES TO ALLOW
THE GRAVES OF VIZNAR TO BE EXHUMED.

Carlos sat back, stunned. Reading quickly through the article he saw that "within the next several weeks, work would begin at the site thought to be the execution place of the famous martyr and twentieth century poet Federico García Lorca and two others."

A dizzying swirl of thoughts began to bombard him. Surely, he thought, this had to have something to do with Nadya's fears and worries. Were they related? He immediately reflected on all the time spent researching without his mind's eye offering a clear picture tying all the events together. These new developments were certainly going to change how Lorca's death was assessed. The Gypsies and the government now added substantial content that could not be ignored. In light of this, Carlos would perhaps need to rethink the approach to his work. It was then that an idea suddenly jumped into his head. If nothing could be gained this evening in talking with Neftali, he would need to go there, to Viznar, and speak to the people in charge of the excavation. Carlos became excited at these new prospects and started formulating in his mind how it could be included in his work. He hesitated, wondering if it would instead be wiser to delay questioning Neftali. But on second thought, he rationalized that perhaps this article in the newspaper, which everyone was sure to have read, could give him an opening for a conversation.

Later that night, Carlos started down the *Paseo de Los Gomerez* enroute to the Albayzin. As usual, the streets were rivers of people navigating toward their homes for supper. He labored in trying to remember his way through the dark narrow streets that brought him to Nadya's house on his previous visit. Soon he started to recognize familiar signs and shortly arrived at the same house from where he remembered hearing the beautiful music. He stood anxiously for a moment before deciding quietly approach the front door. After knocking Carlos looked back at the street lamps and rows of small houses, mostly painted white, that lined the street. After what seemed like an eternity but actually was only a few moments, he nervously decided to knock again. This time, he heard the latch snap and, watching the door slowly open, he saw before him an elderly man slightly hunched over with long gray hair. He wore round, wire-rimmed eyeglasses tightly fit to his round head, which Carlos thought unusually large for his small stature, and his long, straight white hair almost fell to his shoulders. This must be Nadya's grandfather, he thought to himself.

"*Buenas tardes,*" offered Carlos, and the old man's face broke into a smile as he answered softly, "*Buenas noches, muchacho.*"

Carlos was about to present himself when Nadya appeared behind the man—her face radiating a broad smile. Her black shiny hair was tied in a knot with a yellow ribbon and she looked stunning in a simple yellow, sleeveless dress.

"*Carlitos, este es mi abuelo*" (This is my grandfather). Nadya wrapped her hand around the grandfather's elbow, and beckoned for Carlos to enter.

"I am very glad to meet you sir," Carlos replied, holding out his hand, which the old man accepted. Carlos noticed that the man's hands were icy cold.

Nadya motioned for Carlos to follow her while she guided her grandfather slowly toward a leather chair, and at the same time gesturing toward another chair for Carlos to sit alongside him.

"What would you gentlemen like to drink? A glass of wine, beer, or perhaps a soft drink?"

The old man moved his lips although hardly any sound was coming from his mouth, but Nadya understood and repeated a glass of *vino tinto,* red wine. Carlos nodded his head in agreement as she turned, leaving her grandfather and he alone.

"Your city is quite lovely, sir," Carlos ventured.

Carlos' host nodded his head in agreement.

"I heard you play the piano the other evening. It was beautiful, you play quite well."

Nadya's grandfather nodded again, accepting the compliment without saying a word.

Carlos felt the need to continue the conversation despite the old man's reticence. Noticing how distant the man seemed, Carlos guessed him to be over eighty years of age. His eyes scanned the room but did not seem to focus on any one particular thing. Carlos pressed on, settling on the subject of music, which he was hopeful might garner a response:

"In fact, I am listening now mostly to the sounds of Granada, the *Cante Jondo* and *Flamenco*. Neftali invited me the other night to listen to his group of friends perform at their cave … it was utterly sensational."

Nadya's *abuelo's* dark eyes shone, clearly comprehending as he was taking in Carlos' words. His big eyes reminded Carlos of Nadya's, though in appearance, he did not resemble Nadya or Neftali very much. His facial features were bulky, in contrast to the more delicate countenance shared by Nadya and her father—most prominent their tapered jaw lines and noses.

Nadya returned shortly with two glasses of red wine and a small plate of olives and bread, placing them before the two seated men. She announced that her father would join them shortly and that her mother, in the kitchen preparing the supper, would also join everyone as soon as the main meal was served.

Carlos couldn't help but gaze upon Nadya, gliding effortlessly in a saffron-colored dress that accentuated her dancer's body. She was truly the most beautiful girl he had ever seen. Breaking into a wide smile as he looked at his granddaughter, the grandfather's orb-shaped face lit up with delight.

About the same moment, Neftali entered the room with his wife beside him. He was clean-shaven with a ruffled white long-sleeved shirt and his appearance was quite different from that first day Carlos viewed him outside the cave. His wife was petite and slender—like their daughter—and she carried a tray of *tapas*, offering first to the grandfather and then to Carlos.

"*Buenas tardes muchacho* (Good evening) Carlos. What do you think of my daughter? She is a beauty, is she not, *joven* (young man)?"

"Of all the women of Granada, none are as beautiful as your daughter, sir."

Nadya blushed at the compliments and, beaming, her eyes deeply penetrated Carlos.

"You have good taste," Neftali added quietly, taking a sip of the wine Nadya had served him. "I knew there was something special about you the first time I saw you." Carlos felt somewhat embarrassed at the compliment but answered with a quick *"Gracias."*

Another young Gypsy woman Carlos thought to be the household maid entered behind them with a tray of wine and cheese, placing it on a small table between grandfather and Carlos. The old man sat straight in his chair, his eyes moving from person to person. Soon the young maid returned again and motioned to Neftali's wife who then stood up, advising that dinner was ready.

The dining room was cozy, with pictures and photographs of *Flamenco* dancers adorning the walls. The table was set with a white linen cloth and just above, a chandelier with white candles radiated warmth throughout the room. Antique silverware and plates were placed at each setting. The sturdy dining table, together with its matching heavy chairs, was probably a family heirloom, Carlos thought. Neftali asked Carlos to sit at one end of the table while he took the chair on the opposite side. Grandfather and Nadya sat beside one another with Neftali's wife facing them.

The maid brought out a typical Andaluz dish called *sopa de inojo*—fennel soup—served with potatoes and turnips and black *morcilla,* or blood sausage, as an accompaniment. This was followed by fillets of fish covered with an exquisite olive sauce that Carlos had never before tasted and a large salad of greens and sliced fruits mixed together with lemon juice and olive oil. Carlos savored the meal and complimented Neftali's wife, who hardly ate herself but kept rising to refresh the platters of sausage and fried fish. The conversation turned to the caves, tourists and the tremendous heat of the city.

The family was interested in Carlos' impressions of Granada, which he was glad to relate in detail. All the while, Nadya's mother and grandfather observed intently, even as they hardly contributed to the conversation.

The dessert that followed was extraordinary. It was typical Andalusian fare: *toscino del cielo,* a rich flan composed of egg whites, sugar and caramel. *Expréso* was then served in delicate china, and plates of fresh fruit, candied sweets and chocolates were set on the table. All the while, Nadya kept an attentive eye on her grandfather, serving and tending to him.

Neftali next inquired about the progress of Carlos' writing and took great interest in his discussion of Lola and how helpful she was in locating all the materials he was seeking. Finally, Carlos dared to announce what he had been anticipating all evening. "I am almost certainly decided on writing my findings about your poet Lorca in novel form."

Everyone at the table looked at him with little expression on their faces. Nadya turned away, wiping her grandfather's face with her napkin. It was clear to Carlos that he had ventured into a subject that had changed the atmosphere of the table. Continuing ahead as if he were not aware of anything out of place, Carlos said, "Lorca has fascinated me for years and I have spent endless hours in libraries here—reading, researching and talking to anyone who would listen and who might share ideas with me about this great poet. The fact that he was so interested in the music of Granada also prompted me to go further and try and uncover aspects of his life that might not be known to most casual readers." Nadya's mother smiled and stood up to clear the dishes from the table, and grandfather, who had sat quietly throughout the meal, rose to excuse himself. Nadya, standing in unison, assisted him as he ambled from the dining room into the parlor. Neftali, his face betraying nothing out of the ordinary, served a sweet after dinner wine to Carlos and himself.

In a few moments, the sweet sound of a piano commenced, with deliberate, deep notes wafting through the dining room from the adjacent parlor. It was a slow movement Carlos instantly recognized as a Franz Liszt composition—a favorite of his called "Sospiro," a soft, somber piece of music. Carlos knew the old man was the pianist, and commented to Neftali, "I heard him play the other evening; he is quite good, don't you think?" Neftali smiled and nodded his head in agreement.

Nadya had since returned and sat by Carlos at the table, listening along with them for several minutes. She turned to Carlos, saying, "Grandfather is mostly quiet; he hardly speaks, but seems to express himself through his music, and he enjoys playing late into the night."

When he finished the piece, there was a silence throughout the house.

"Shall we go in the garden and have a cognac?" asked Neftali in a soft voice, breaking the quiet of the moment.

The three moved through the parlor where grandfather sat looking at the keys of the piano, his hands folded in his lap. He nodded his head, neither looking up nor acknowledging their presence as they passed by. Entering the garden on this warm, beautiful night, the music began once again. Grandfather began to play the second movement of the same Liszt piece Carlos immediately recognized. For some reason, he had dared not broach the subject of what he had read in the newspaper. That would have to wait until another time.

# CHAPTER 20

F EDERICO STEPPED OFF the train. It was twenty minutes of
eight in the morning. His eyes searched the surrounding area to
see if the lizard was anywhere to be seen. He looked haggard and
disheveled, dressed in loose-fitting overalls buttoned up the front. His
hair, hung wildly in front of his face and two days growth of beard lent
him a desperate look of someone who was being hunted.

He lit a cigarette as he stepped onto the platform searching for
his family, who were due to meet him here at the station. He smiled
and relaxed when he saw his sister and mother approaching him from
the far end of the platform. Doña Vincenta showered her son with
hugs and kisses, glad to see he had arrived safely. Federico kissed them
without really seeing their faces. He was tired and distraught from his
overnight ride where he had slept little, imagining all the horrors that
might befall him. He was exhausted but he was glad to be home.

Together, the three loaded his suitcases into their waiting car and
headed off to their summer home in the southeastern extreme of the
city, the *Huerta de San Vincente*. This was the home Don Vincente,
Federico's father, had chosen for the cool breezes that swept this city
quarter in the night.

Arriving home, Lorca's father greeted him with hugs and kisses, happy as always that Federico was here with family to celebrate their Saints day. Angelina, the maid and nanny for Federico's sister's children who had cared for him since he was little, threw her arms around him in greeting.

The Lorca family preferred to remain detached from the news of the day. The uprising that the papers was reporting appeared to be some far away event.

It was July 17 and Granada would be one of the first cities to join the rebellion a few days later, on July 20. Nightly reports from General Quiepo de Llanos from Sevilla exhorted the Spanish communities to join this mutiny for the good of Spain, for God and for the *Patria*, the Fatherland. Federico spent most of the month here at the *Huerta*, writing and enjoying his family … recounting to them all his projects and travels and new ideas for plays he was in the midst of developing. These were happy and uncertain times; though they were also times to reacquaint with old friends. His closest friends, glad to welcome him back home, came and visited. Several advised him of the dangers and perils that existed in Granada. These warnings always put Federico in a state of fright. Often, he would remain isolated in his room until coaxed out by his family. A few friends urged Federico to abandon Granada and seek refuge in another, safer location; but he disregarded their advice. It weighed on him; he heard all their pleas, but their words had little meaning. He was tone deaf to their urgent requests to escape. Why would he be threatened? What had he done?

Lorca knew his family had stature and he could not be convinced to try and run in the night to a safe Republican zone, though many of Federico's friends escaped to these safe places through the mountains of Granada to the Republican zones that surrounded the city. Shortly after the commencement of the rebellion, Loyalist airplanes dropped bombs on the rebel city for two straight weeks, attempting to quell the revolt at its roots.

The thought of being alone in between two places—one where he felt safe and the other an unknown, without anyone to rely on — terrified him. He had never been someone who was able to spend very much time alone. He needed to be surrounded by admirers with whom he was assured of appreciation and affection.

He worked and wrote, looking for an escape from everything happening around him. He remembered all the wonderful days he had spent writing here. His much-acclaimed plays, *Yerma* and *Bodas de Sangre*, were conceived here in the *Huerta*. He read the papers, which disturbed him, as he did not comprehend the scope of the terror that was surrounding him.

Preoccupied with his own safety, he smoked incessantly, and was barely able to sleep. A constant foreboding was growing within him as he grew more and more fearful and less sure of his decision to return to Granada.

One day, two men came to the *Huerta* looking for the brother of the caretaker of the Lorca house. He was out and not satisfied to find him absent they decided to abuse his brother whom they were sure was hiding him. They pulled him from the small house where the gardeners lived that was connected by a small walkway to the Lorca *Huerta*. They tied him to a post outside the Lorca residence and proceeded to beat him with a whip. Federico was outraged at this violation in front of his own home and moved to intervene. One of the men grabbed his arm and slapped him in the face, knocking Federico to the ground. As he lay there looking up the man shouted, "We know who you are, you goddamn queer; be careful, for we may come back for you." It was clear that the rebels were aware of Lorca's renewed presence in the city and they were not happy with it. His outspokenness on many issues was well-known in his hometown. His quirky behavior and repute as a homosexual followed him here and was not well-received in this bastion of conservatism. They also accused him of being a communist. His sexual behavior and his unorthodox writings were viewed by many as anti-Catholic and were sufficient cause to make him numerous enemies.

That evening, the Lorca family sat quietly at dinner. The discussion centered on Federico. What to do? Finally, after contemplating several alternatives, it was decided that he should not stay on any longer at the *Huerta*. He had to be moved to somewhere where there was no danger.

Finally, the poet's father said, "In the home of our friends Rosales, there he will be safe."

Luis Rosales was a poet of some fame in Granada — a good friend of the Lorca family, who had known Federico for some time. In addition, he was from a deeply-rooted Falangist family and his brother José was a district director of the organization. The three brothers were zealous Falangists and were aware that the poet was coming to stay with them for his own protection. They did not think his stature as a poet was something that would be of interest to the rebellion, nor did they believe that they were hiding him. He was simply a guest in their home. Luis and his father were people who could be trusted by the Lorca family.

The Falangist Rosales brothers were whole-hearted enthusiasts of the new revolt against the elected Republican government — the left-leaning Popular Front — and if they offered protection to Federico, he was sure to be safe. The family was comprised mainly of stern Catholics who believed that this new democratic government was sending Spain toward ruin.

Don Vincente García Rodriguez, Federico's father, was friendly with Luis' father and both had always shared much more liberal tendencies than the rest of the Rosales family. The two elders had known each other for many years and had some mutual financial concerns. Federico's father was sure they would agree to harbor Federico for any time needed. The event that sealed their decision to move Federico was the receipt of a letter sent to him without return address. It threatened the life of the poet. Federico trembled as he read this and for the next several days, as was usual when he was frightened, remained in his room without eating—terrified of the unfolding events. That same day, Federico's father made the call to the Rosales' home.

The Rosales family car arrived at the Lorca *Huerta* almost immediately to take Federico to their home on *Calle Angulo,* behind the Catedral and near the police station on *Calle Duquesa.* This, Granada's old city, was situated just off the *Gran Via* in the central part of the city. It was August 9, almost a full month since Federico had arrived here in Granada. It was decided Federico would remain there until everyone was assured of the intentions of these new authorities. Stories of daily executions and reprisals circulated freely. The city of Granada and the Lorca family were frozen with fear.

# CHAPTER 21

F RANCI HEREDIA HAD spent days poking around the Albayzin and he had uncovered sufficient information through his network of friends that there was indeed a plan brewing to locate Lorca's grave with the goal of collecting his remains. He was stumped though as to any good reason for doing so and why Inspector De Los Rios would have so much interest in something like this. He was, after all, usually attached to cases of the highest level, like the smuggling of drugs from Morocco or the illicit prostitution rings that were sprouting up throughout Andalucia. But, digging up the bones of a dead poet who, these days, was considered a legend — as well as a tourist symbol attracting people to Granada — he could not comprehend.

Franci now needed to know which Gypsy was going to handle it. After that, he would be free of the inspector and could finally return to his usual routine. He assumed that whoever undertook this deed knew about *Fuente Grande,* the reputed olive grove where Lorca and several others, including two *bandilleros* from the bullring and a respected school teacher, were taken and executed outside the village of Viznar on the road to Alfacar. If someone was going to steal Lorca's bones, they would have to be familiar with the site and the security it was sure to have. He formulated a plan to spend the next several evenings near the site and see who might show up. He would then report this to the inspector and his task would be completed.

Later that evening, after the sun had set, Franci mounted his *moto*, a small 125cc model, and set out to the northeast of Granada in the direction of Alfacar, which was located some eight or nine kilometers away. It was an unpaved secondary road with many potholes and bumps that turned a normally short trip into one that lasted him the better part of an hour. He arrived at the desolate spot and noted that there was a large area cordoned off with a yellow rope and a number of signs warning tourists and passersby not to intrude into it. He found a stand of pine trees some one hundred meters up an adjacent hill—a perfect place to hide his *moto* and where he would have a good vantage point from which to view any visitors that might show up. He sat down behind a large pine tree on a bed of soft pine needles and lit a cigarette. Now all he could do was wait.

Franci waited until the moon had disappeared from the sky, at which point he could barely maintain a view of the area he was watching. After midnight, he decided to call it quits. Not a single vehicle or person had passed by and it became clear to him that no one was going to show. He second-guessed himself, thinking that this whole endeavor could be for nothing. Disgusted, he collected the number of cigarette butts he had smoked, stuffed them in his pocket, and mounted his *moto* for the bumpy ride back to Granada.

Franci repeated this routine for three more nights without any luck and was ready to abandon the plan. It was then that he thought of the detective. Going back to De Los Rios empty handed, without anything meaningful to report, was out of the question. He decided to make one final attempt. After that, he would report to the inspector that if there was a plot in the air, he could not find out who the culprits were.

Franci, under the same pine tree as always, had to pinch himself to stay awake, but finally dozed off—his head resting against the trunk of his hiding place. But suddenly, with a gasp, he awoke for some reason. How long had he been asleep? He had been awakened by the sound of a car door slamming. Franci was groggy, but managed to get to his knees and peered out from behind his sheltered spot to see what was happening below. At this time of night there was hardly any vigilance applied in guarding the cordoned-off site. He knew an occasional watchman passed by to check for intruders, but was certain that occurred mainly in the daylight hours. He heard several men talking below. There must have been at least three or four men in all. From his perch, he could see their silhouette-like outlines but could not make out any faces. They were walking around the area with flashlights, talking in hushed tones, apparently checking out the area. He knew then he needed to get closer to catch a glimpse of the intruders. Franci looked around, surveying the setting around him, and knowing there was no way to approach from where he was situated without being heard or noticed. So he just knelt, staring into the darkness and listening to the low voices of the men — frustrated that his plan was so inept.

With the notable exception of his bad luck with the inspector, Franci lived a somewhat charmed life and, in this particular moment, luck once again decided to smile on him. A single man returned to the vehicle and opened the door, the light from the interior of the car shining directly on his face. Franci recognized him instantly and searched his memory for his name. What was it? Nestar? . . . Nazareno? . . . Nino? . . . What was it? He had seen him many times before.

Neftali? ... Neftali? Yes, that was it! — a Gypsy who owned a *Flamenco* cave. Franci faded behind the pine tree smiling to himself, knowing that he had not been seen. The inspector would be happy to receive this news. After all that had transpired, the end game was now up to De Los Rios. Franci's job was finished. He breathed a deep sigh as he waited for the men to climb back into their auto and drive away. He remained in place for several minutes until he was sure their car was far enough away not to notice him. Standing up, Franci traced his steps back through the woods to where his *moto* was hidden, kick started the engine, and trekked back toward the city.

# CHAPTER 22

CARLOS SAT AND wondered what Nadya had confided in him about. The headlines in the daily paper jumped out at him:

WORK TO BEGIN AT THE LORCA SITE NEAR VIZNAR

The government commission of Granada announced today that the final arrangements had been made to excavate the site where the renowned poet, Federico García Lorca, is assumed to have been executed along with several other comrades. The Lorca family has finally granted permission and lifted the remaining barriers and objections previously made. They were allowing the exhumation to go forward.

Carlos knew that this would cause great concern in the city. For one, Granada had been the first Spanish city where the mutiny had begun and was successful. For another, it was a conservative city and many of its citizens still lamented the death of Franco and Granada's return to a more democratic government. Old rivalries and fears were sure to begin anew. In addition, many old questions would resurface. Who actually was responsible for Lorca's death, and who had given the final order? Who were the men who took him to the hillside to be executed? What new honors would be bestowed on the deceased poet if his remains were found?

Many thought this was a true waste of government resources. Numerous streets and avenues throughout the country were being renamed, erasing previous honors bestowed to the rebel victors. The famous *Valle de Los Caidos*, Valley of the Fallen, where Generalissimo Franco's remains were entombed, was stripped of its importance as the new government attempted to rectify history. Old agreements that all this brutal history be swept under the rug were once again brought out into the light of day for reexamination and perusal. This new attempt to airbrush history was rubbing many people—*important* people—the wrong way.

Carlos thought it would be an appropriate time to approach Nadya so that together they might approach her father about Nadya's fears and this controversy over Lorca's bones. So here he sat, as always, in the same small restaurant in the *Plaza Nueva,* awaiting her arrival and hoping to discuss these headlines and how they might relate to her father. A few minutes later, she appeared, walking down the *Paseo*—her tall, olive figure standing out from the crowd—as beautiful and radiant as ever. Spying Carlos, she flashed a broad smile and greeted him—kissing both his cheeks.

"Let's sit; I want to show you something I think you should see," Carlos began. He reached across the table for the newspaper and opened it in front of her, revealing the unsettling headlines. Nadya pulled the paper closer and started intently reading the Lorca story. When she finished, she looked up at Carlos and with an anguished look asked simply, "What do you think we ought to do?"

"I think we should go to your father and confront him or at least ask him anyway," Carlos replied.

"However, I must say he doesn't know I talked to you about this whole thing—you are not a Gypsy and he will be very disappointed in learning that I have shared something that happened in the cave with you. Gypsies are a closed group—we have always kept matters to ourselves and it's possible my father might refuse to discuss anything with us at all."

"Well ... he will as soon as we go together and tell him that it was I who goaded you into telling me. He knows we've been seeing a lot of each other and it would be natural for me to recognize if something were eating at you. I'd also say I heard something in the cave that evening when those men didn't realize I was right behind them. It is possible that I learned something of their discussion as a result. Shall we agree then that we can talk to your father? After all, he knows my keen interest in the work I'm doing about Lorca. I really don't think it's strange that I show concern and anyway, it might be worth a try. What do you think?"

The two of them decided that in the evening, they would go to the cave. There was no *espectaculo* that night and Neftali would be there preparing for the upcoming weekend.

# CHAPTER 23

FRANCI HEREDIA SAT in the inspector's office, waiting for him to finish a telephone call. When De Los Rios hung up the receiver, he stood up, nodded at Franci and greeted the Gypsy with the same insincere smile he always reserved for him.

"So, amigo, what have we found out about our friends from the Albayzin?" Franci related to him his tactics of the previous several days while the inspector lit a cigarette, listening intently to the narrative Franci was weaving for him. Franci told De Los Rios of his several visits to the gravesite and how he was almost ready to give up when a group of Gypsies suddenly appeared on his fourth attempt. When he recognized the Gypsy who seemed to be the leader of the group, Franci watched the inspector's face turn somber. This surprised Franci, as he had expected instead to witness him beaming with delight. However, De Los Rios' initial response radiated deep concern. The inspector paced across the room without saying a word. Stopping by the window, he stared at the street below for a long while. Franci squirmed in his chair, uncomfortable with this unanticipated reception on the inspector's part.

"*Señor*, are you alright? You look a bit worried. Is something wrong? Are you not pleased with the way I handled this? I could not think of anything else to do but to go there. I figured if the rumors were true, someone would *have* to show up at the site."

"*Si, amigo,* you did the right thing. It was very clever of you. I was just thinking back to a time many years ago." The inspector turned around abruptly and faced Franci.

"I am fine … now I need to do my part. Like always, Franci, I knew I could depend on you."

Franci rose from his chair, realizing the session was over. Intuitively, he always harbored the unpleasant belief he would be back in this chair again when the inspector came up short. He didn't feel at all satisfied in the way the inspector responded. Maybe it was just time to move on and start over again somewhere else. Sensing his anxiety, De Los Rios moved closer to Franci, putting his hand on his shoulder to comfort him — "Don't worry, *amigo,* you have done what I have asked of you. I am sure I won't need your services any time soon. Gracias. Go home and forget about this thing. The summer is almost over and you probably have a lot to do."

The words rang hollow in Franci's ears as he departed the office, slipping down the staircase and trying to go unnoticed by the people who always were milling about the station. He was convinced his luck would run out sooner or later. He shuddered to think of the consequences if he were discovered to be a renegade Gypsy. Moving into the street, he headed back toward the Albayzin, wondering when and where this whole episode would end. He knew that the inspector was tenacious and that no good could come of it.

Fearing again that it was just a matter of time until he was found out, Franci reached into his pocket for a cigarette and started up the hill. The coming day was promising to be oppressively hot once again and as he walked, the perspiration streamed down his face.

# CHAPTER 24

CARLOS AND NADYA sat together against the cave's wall in two chairs tourists were typically seated in. A young man served them cups of Manzanilla tea and some sweet cakes. Nadya was sitting apprehensively next to Carlos, anticipating the arrival of her father, whom she had advised she and Carlos would be visiting that night. Neftali emerged from behind the red curtain that led to the kitchen, smiling as if he anticipated something quite different was about to happen.

*"Buenas tardes muchachos. ¿De que les debo esta visita?"* (To what do I owe this visit?)

Nadya gave a quick glance at Carlos, who sat looking directly at Neftali. Without hesitation, Carlos started to explain the reason for his visit to the cave that evening. The Gypsy sat quietly for approximately fifteen minutes while Carlos recounted all of the couple's reasons for requesting this audience. He spoke anxiously but did not hesitate to tell Neftali of his daughter's fears, all of the recent interest in the newspapers headlines about the poet Lorca, and what they had overheard that night in this very cave.

The Gypsy sat stoically, showing no emotion, while he intently listened to Carlos' story. When Carlos had finished, Neftali turned and looked at his daughter. There was no recrimination in his face. He then turned to Carlos and softly said, *"Joven,* you are very intelligent and insightful. I am sure that all your investigations will lead to something very grand. From the first time we met, I felt you had a special sentiment for Granada and for Lorca. You know my daughter has shared with you something that should not be made known to anyone who is not of our blood. But, I also recognize that this is all behind us, so let me tell you what it is you have come seeking from this old Gypsy.

"I had hoped you were going to bring me happy news — news of two young people who had a special feeling for each other and who had come to ask permission from the head of the family that they might formalize their relationship, as is the custom of our people. But instead, you have come to me with something unexpected, and I see that I have no alternative but to explain to you things you may not understand."

Neftali leaned back in his seat, took his tobacco pouch from his pocket and rolled a cigarette. He started talking slowly, looking directly at Carlos and then at Nadya. The smoke from his cigarette hung in the air all about them as Neftali recounted his tale.

"Federico García Lorca was, as I have told you many times, someone who understood the Gypsies. His collection of poems, *Romancero Gitano,* endeared him to us for eternity, as he was one who understood the soul of the Gypsy. How, I do not know, but it is certain that he had a special connection to our plight. That conflict that every man has — between what he desires on a day-to-day level, and what he knows his soul desires — Lorca understood. It is a separation — between man and his daily routine and the time he has free to reflect on his life and recognize the reality that exists. It is when he understands the hardships he must deal with, the brutality of daily life, and the dreams he had always hoped would come true that he now knows will never be realized.

"Why Lorca, the son of a wealthy landowner, was able to capture our being, I again say I cannot tell you. Other times, I have commented to you that he belonged to us, the Gypsies. It was he who brought us out of oblivion by recreating our songs and assuring us that we were worth remembering. He knew the *Cante Jondo*, the songs of Andalucia that give meaning to our often difficult existence. He knew Granada owed us more. We were being commercialized and cheapened and Lorca brought us back to ourselves by rejecting anything that he did not see as pure, as original.

"Now, you ask me about what you have overheard, and I can tell you it is true. A group of us have decided that it is necessary to retrieve the bones of Lorca, so that we can put to rest once and for all the doubt about his murder—and so that those who committed this heinous act will rest, also knowing that their secret is safe, and that no one will know their identities. Yes, we know their secret. We know the men who took him from the Rosales home to the *estacion de policia*, and I can tell you that they were cowards without orders from anyone. They acted purely out of personal vendettas and vengeance.

"You may ask what will be accomplished by our act. I can tell you that it will bring finality to this whole yet unwritten episode. The government will see the lies of those fascists who have recounted this death story to them. New questions will arise as to his death, and the myth of Federico will continue. Is it possible that you can understand what I am telling you?"

Carlos and Nadya sat stunned at the story just told to them. Neither was able to add to or question anything Neftali had poured from his soul. They could only stare at each other quizzically. Carlos ventured, "And how do you suppose to get to the poet with all the surveillance—especially with all the *reportajes* appearing daily in the local newspapers and on television? The interest in Lorca has never been so intense."

Neftali smiled, stood up and wished them a good evening, without addressing Carlos' question. Instead, he began telling them that there was a street vendor some fifty meters down the *Paseo* who had fried sardines and green peppers and that they should be sure to stop there as his fare was superb, and it was not often that he appeared in this neighborhood.

Carlos thanked Neftali for his frankness and suddenly felt a warm affection for the old man he had not previously experienced. Nadya kissed her father and embraced him tightly before she and Carlos turned toward the street. Walking down the hill hand-in-hand, the couple soon came upon the vendor her father had described and, sitting on a wall by the River Darro, enjoyed sardines cooked on an open flame. They had also purchased two bottles of cold beer that complemented the meal perfectly. The lighted Alhambra above watched over them as they relaxed and marveled at the beauty of the moonrise.

Nadya felt that a weight had been lifted from her and she laughed and ate as the water from the Rio Darro rushing by them below drowned out their chatter and laughter. She and Carlos kissed passionately in the warm Granada evening. In the back of Carlos's mind, he was filled with anticipation at what the next few days would bring.

# CHAPTER 25

C ARLOS' STUDIES NOW concentrated only on the final days and hours of the poet. He was beginning to truly understand the toxic atmosphere that existed in Granada when Lorca returned there from Madrid. He read many accounts of the proceedings of that time, in which everyone recounted differently the players and their actions during the last few days Lorca was in Granada. Lorca was now becoming more than just a topic for Carlos; he was an obsession — an obsession that now made Carlos a participant in this narrative without any idea of its outcome. The days he was spending locked up in the library with stacks of books and newspaper accounts were coming to an end as Carlos realized that the novel was now something he was immersed in. The utter insanity that Granada was in those final days of the poet's life must have been like the turmoil he was feeling now. The puzzle pieces he needed to conclude his book were starting to fall into place and Carlos knew he was playing a role in the finale. For Carlos, the confessions of Neftali brought Lorca to life within him.

Federico had no idea when he left Madrid on the evening of July 16 that the very next day, the mutiny would begin in North Africa. It would only take a few days to spread to Sevilla and then quickly to

Granada, from where the Granada military command took its orders. Two lower-level army officers, Lieutenant Pelayo of the Civil Guard and Captain Nestares of the infantry had the loyalty of their men and backed the Nationalist rebel forces led by General Quiepo de Llano of Sevilla. They concealed this from their commanding officer who had remained loyal to the elected Republican government. Without any resistance from the military or the Civil Guard, these units covertly supported the uprising and assumed control of the brigade. The takeover of Granada was completed in just a few days. Their commander, a veteran army officer, had no idea of the treachery of his subordinates. Completely surprised, he was relieved from his command, arrested and finally transported and executed for his refusal to support the rebels.

On July 20 most of the newly elected Civil Government of Granada, which had recently gone into session, was arrested and detained in the central jail. The rebels quickly moved to eliminate any opposition. In early August, the bloodshed began. Summarily, without trials or any due process, these officials were taken to the cemetery near the Alhambra and executed. Over the course of the next few months, hundreds of loyalists would be taken away in truckloads. People were afraid to come out of their homes when, each morning before dawn, the sound of the truck engines labored up the hill toward the cemetery.

Among the executed was the brother-in-law of Federico, Manuel Fernandez Montesinos, a doctor and socialist who had been elected the new *alcalde*, or mayor. Realizing his plight, he requested that his local priest give him last rites and this wish was granted. He was only thirty-five years of age and left behind his wife—Federico's sister—and three small children.

The city was now in chaos and the only real resistance came from the Albayzin, where streets were blockaded and trenches dug by the loyalists to slow the advance of the militia. The superior power of the military naturally prevailed. The rebels mounted canons from the heights of the Alhambra and quickly subdued the resistance of the poorly armed citizens. It was a one sided battle. Many loyalists were dragged into the streets and shot outside their homes. Men, women and children were indiscriminately murdered.

One of the largest worker demonstrations organized by the syndicate associations and the political left had recently been staged through the streets of Granada. Most of those who marched came from the poorer neighborhoods of the city like the Albayzin where living the conditions were appalling. The organizers were systematically hunted down by the soldiers and executed.

It was surprising to Carlos that the newly elected officials, realizing the growing danger from informants, did little to either protect themselves or move to arm the citizenry when it was within their power to do so. There was ample time to accomplish this, and it proved to be a most tragic and deadly oversight. Carlos could not fathom any reason for this reluctance with so much advance warning from the events in Sevilla and Africa. Carlos felt anger and frustration as he sat in the library, comprehending the consequences of this fatal error.

The battle between the rebels and loyalists was over before it started and as a result, Granada fell into the camp of the rebellious soldiers. Now, it was time for reprisals.

The new Civil Governor of Granada, José Valdez Guzman, a career military officer who joined the rebel cause early on, drew up lists of those who opposed, or whom they expected to oppose this new regime. He personally took charge of the repression that befell the city for the next six months. University professors, newspaper editors, musicians, lawyers, labor organizers, and people from almost every profession were taken daily to the cemetery in Granada and shot—forcing their grieving relatives to come later to identify the corpses. In fact, so many were executed there that the bodies were buried atop each other in mass graves, making identification difficult.

Federico had always detested the political parties, declaring himself a revolutionary, as were all true poets. He never considered himself siding with any politician. He dined often in Madrid with José Primo de Rivera, the founder of the right-wing Falangist party in Spain. The

Falangist leader was a great admirer of Lorca's poetry and considered him a valued friend. Lorca's companions were a mixture of those of the right and of the left. These friends tried resolutely to coax the poet to their own particular leanings, but Lorca always laughed them off, refusing be pulled into the politics.

At this time, the political situation was changing rapidly. Spain had moved from a dictatorship to a conservative parliamentary government, to a socialist-dominated system in just six years. Lorca had signed many anti-fascist petitions, as did most of the intellectuals and artists expressing their support for the working classes and the deplorable conditions under which they lived. His heart and mind were with the underprivileged, even as he came from a wealthy family.

The constant, underlying theme Lorca had expressed in his poetry and plays pointed to the plight of the common man—the suffering that he endured in surviving the harsh culture and institutions that were part of his daily life. The unjust role of women in Spain, who were seen as inferior in their defined role as mother and housekeeper, was a constant topic Lorca repeatedly revisited. As a result, his productions were seen as obscene and heretical by the standards of conservative Spain. The usual topics Lorca touched upon, such as marriage and the church, were considered taboo in this most traditional country. The church detested his willingness and keen ability to question the sacred values and institutions Lorca openly exposed in his works.

However, everyone familiar with Lorca knew—except those with deep hatred of his artistic portrayals, which they considered out of bounds—that Lorca never involved himself in political activities or philosophies. He was, most fundamentally, an artist.

Lorca, in his daily life, had a deep love for his country and its institutions. He was a devout Catholic and marched in religious processions he thought beautiful and unique to Spain. He truly did not see his work as a condemnation of Spain, but rather as an expression of artistic freedom, challenging ideas and institutions that had never previously been doubted.

Once, in a newspaper interview expressing his opinion about the fall of Granada in 1492 to the Spanish monarchs, he used the poorest possible choice of words — ones that would eventually come back to haunt him. The poet characterized the defeat and expulsion of the Moors in one short sentence:

*"One of the greatest civilizations in every aspect was washed away remaining only a wasteland populated by the worst bourgeoisie in Spain today."*

These words quickly reached the ears of the conspirators and reactionaries who would soon seize control of the city of Granada. They were words that would not be forgotten. After all, Lorca's fame and notoriety as a poet and playwright preceded him. He had attained great renown throughout the world, so that word of his arrival in Granada was published in the daily newspaper the day after his arrival.

Federico felt more at ease. The Rosales family was well known and, due to their involvement with the rebellion, men came and went with regularity during the days Lorca stayed with them. Federico was often at the Rosales piano, entertaining the women of the family. He recited verse both from his recent plays and poems, much to their delight. He also sang songs from his time in New York, as well as Gypsy tunes of Granada. He was a natural performer and the Rosales women adored him. He was so enthralling that Andrés Segovia, the famed guitarist, had watched in amazement as Lorca performed one evening at the apartment of a wealthy New Yorker who had invited both of the men there to meet their friends. Never had Segovia seen such a talented performer captivate his audience so completely.

Federico now spent long hours working, writing and thinking of new projects. Many hours were spent with Luis, his poet friend and host, discussing a new book of poetry that Lorca was about to publish. But the daily air raids by the Republican side caused him tremendous anxiety and he would remain stricken for hours, hiding in his room until coaxed down by the Rosales women, who invited him to join them for tea and cakes. He knew his brother-in-law was jailed and always felt himself in a state of constant panic. As it happened, the length of his stay at the Rosales home would be only one short week.

# CHAPTER 26

N EFTALI AND THREE Gypsies exited the cave and climbed into the old blue Spanish Seat parked nearby. It was early evening as they started the motor of the blue, vintage auto, whose two rear doors opened in an opposite fashion of those in the front. The car slowly pulled away and headed down the hill, out of the Albayzin. At the same time, a small dark Renault with two male passengers in dark clothes started its engine and began to follow the Seat down the narrow streets leading to central city. They kept a safe enough distance behind so as not to be noticed. The first car wended its way through the streets of the central city, heading north — the direction the pursuing car had expected. Arriving at the intersection of the *autovias* that could take travelers in any direction from central Granada, the first car chose the route traversing in a northwesterly direction toward Madrid. The second auto slowed and the men inside looked at each other quizzically. They had orders to follow these men toward the northeast where Viznar was situated. Then, they were to report immediately to the inspector that indeed the Gypsies were in route to their anticipated arrival point. But to their surprise, the car was heading in a different direction. The men pulled the Renault to the side of the road and radioed to police headquarters. The call was quickly forwarded to Inspector De Los Rios, who listened carefully to the details of the news without expression. He knew that the poor system of roads in Granada would not allow them any other access from their present location to Viznar. He relayed his orders into the receiver quietly, "Wait there for one half hour and if they return, follow them."

He hung up the telephone and pondered what was happening—he knew from experience that sooner or later, events would unravel. Most often, detective work did not reveal much in the first instance. De Los Rios sat at his desk, thinking for a moment and then shuffling through the mountain of papers resting on it.

After waiting for what seemed a reasonable time for their prey to appear, the two detectives started the engine and headed back toward Granada. Their anticipated catch had not returned.

For the next six hours, the Gypsies negotiated the two-lane highway from Granada to Madrid and finally had arrived at their destination several hours before daybreak. The men stepped out of the car into the countryside on the outskirts of Madrid proper—shivering a bit as they were unaccustomed to the cool night air of the north. They opened the trunk of their auto, extracting flashlights and the few tools they needed to complete their task. Neftali spoke quietly to the assembled men, giving assurances and orders that were obeyed quickly. He then removed from the trunk of the car some gloves and a small canvas bag. The men huddled together to receive some final instructions and proceeded up the small hill. When they arrived at their destination, one man remained behind while the others opened the gate and entered the open dark area—their flashlights shining on the narrow stone path, as the few dim streetlights outside did not provide sufficient light for the men to see their way into the enclosure. From there, they headed off in different directions, closely following Neftali's instructions. Neftali took his flashlight and started to examine his surroundings, looking first at the rows of all-white structures with inscriptions engraved on their compartments. He bent over with his face close to his light examining the inscriptions. He moved along quickly, examining each location carefully. Unsuccessful, he passed by the first row of structures. The second group yielded a similarly fruitless search. He shined his light first on the bottom row and then the top row—resting two meters above him—intently trying to discern the names of each compartment. Again, he failed to find the name he had come for. As he moved toward the third set of concrete encasements, he heard a low, shrill whistle about twenty or thirty meters away, and quickly stopped what he was doing to move in that direction. He arrived seconds later where his two companions were pointing toward one of the vaults. Neftali shined his light on the inscription from where the Gypsy had been pointing. The chiseled letters in the concrete spelled

DOÑA VINCENTA LORCA ROMERO, 1870-1959

*Que en Paz Descanse* ... May she rest in peace.

They were at the tomb of Federico's mother. Spanish cemeteries for years have not buried their dead underground, as was the custom in most countries. Instead, they built pantheons, or rows of niches stacked one upon another where families regularly came to leave flowers and offerings on the shelves provided for each niche.

Quickly, Neftali started to work with the tools he had brought. Two men assisted him as they worked hurriedly, intent on the task before them. They worried that some passerby might detect the sounds of their work, although it was late at night and the probable chance of being caught was slim. But in just a matter of seconds, Neftali took the canvas bag and brought it closer to where they were working, choosing among the tools. The simple task was complete. Neftali finished and put everything back in place, rearranging the flowers so it appeared nothing had been disturbed. The men returned quickly to the gate where the waiting sentry told them that all was quiet and normal. They walked quickly in the cool night air, back down the hill to their auto.

Neftali lit another cigarette and breathed in, looking all around at the dark outlines surrounding him. He smiled and thought to himself that they had done well and everything had worked out according to plan. The auto's diesel engine started and the vehicle progressed toward the *autovia* for the long trip back to Granada.

The sun had just come up in the eastern sky and the city was just beginning to awaken when the Seat reached home. The occupants of the car bid each other good day, glad that they were back at home before heading off in their separate directions. The morning air was heavy, promising yet another hot Andalusian summer day.

# CHAPTER 27

WITH HIS FOREFINGER, Carlos lightly outlined the length of Nadya's beautifully sculpted profile, and drew circles around her eyes. He then ran his hands through her long, black, silky hair, gently touching her ears just beneath. Nadya murmured slightly, responding to his gentle strokes — partly asleep, but awake enough to feel the caresses. He next ran his hand down her lithe body, delighting in her curves and contented warmth.

It had been almost a month since they first made love — a volcanic encounter where there were no boundaries expressed. They each sought to know the intimate desires of their partner and when they discovered a particular ecstasy that each enjoyed, threw themselves into it without shame or reservation. They enjoyed a sweet love that only poets write of and to which Carlos responded with his total heart. Carlos knew this to be the special love he had always hoped for and he could not imagine even a single day without this sweet Gypsy at his side. Even as the heat of August was intolerable, Nadya enjoyed coming to the Hotel Alixares next to the Alhambra for the breezes that passed through the mountain-top hotel throughout the night.

These past weeks proved to be a whirlwind for Carlos, as during most days, Nadya would accompany him to the libraries of Granada. She would sit patiently while he labored on this project he had fully immersed himself in. He wondered often if he would *ever* be able to finish. He toyed with the idea of abandoning his novel to write yet another history of the poet's death, but reasoned that it would be difficult to add anything significant to the murky last few days of Lorca's life. Despite the closeness he felt toward Lorca, the Gypsies, detective De Los Rios and all the intrigue, he was having difficulty finding a satisfying end to his work. So confusing were the last days of the famous poet that anything factual would appear as sheer conjecture and would probably be contested by the multitude of authors already published on the subject.

The testimony of those who were clearly involved when Lorca was taken from the headquarters and executed was both contradictory and inconclusive at best. Carlos had read the scores of interviews and letters provided by Lola involving persons who were near to Lorca—either friend or foe. But there was no definitive accounting of events other than when he was sequestered and shortly thereafter, executed.

Most evenings, Carlos would join Nadya at the *cueva* as he never tired in his delight of watching her body respond to the music of *Flamenco*. She always seemed energized by the music, despite attending the club those many weeks throughout the busy summer season when it was at its busiest.

There had been little news of Neftali's plans for exhuming Lorca. Both Carlos and Nadya hoped that Neftali might not do something he would later regret. The government, according the newspapers, was now constructing walls around the perimeter of the supposed site of the execution in Viznar. From the photographs in the papers, they appeared to be constructed of plastic cloth with iron poles dug in every two or three meters. And more security was likely to be added as well. A new article would appear daily in the papers covering the reaction to the government's decision to open up old wounds. It had even been said that there was possibility of a violent response. Everyone in Granada was keenly sensitive to what was happening in Viznar.

Carlos believed that the best term to describe the situation was fear. There were hundreds of sites such as this but few with one as famous as Lorca. Many exhumations in communities throughout Spain were already underway and to identify remains was a long and tedious process. In some sites, the expectation was to recover ten to fifteen remains, though once commenced, the exhumations yielded considerably more bodies than originally anticipated. Once this process had begun in earnest, hundreds of requests to open locations began pouring into the government. There were communities where the local citizenry knew of such sites, but who had not yet stepped forward to inform the authorities for fear of reprisal.

Carlos sat up next to Nadya, contemplating all that was happening. It was all so complicated, but good food for his novel. Nadya began to stir. She opened her large dark eyes and a smile followed as it always did when she was near him. He bent over and kissed her softly on the lips. She put her arm around his neck and pulled him closer. It was late morning and Carlos had promised the librarian Lola he would be there to peruse the few resources he had guessed may have been overlooked. Nadya also needed to attend to affairs at the cave.

They both showered and dressed quickly and descended the stairs to the main lobby of the hotel. They were greeted by all the morning personnel who knew Carlos and were now becoming acquainted with his nighttime visitor. The couple moved toward the exit, where the usual number of tourists awaiting entrance to the Alhambra queued. Carlos signaled to the first available taxi and once Nadya was safely aboard, handed the driver some pesetas. As the taxi departed, Carlos headed down the *Paseo do Los Gomerez* for what he hoped would be a short day in the library. But he could not possibly have anticipated what waited for him when he arrived later that evening at the hotel.

# CHAPTER 28

I T WAS LATE when Carlos arrived back at Alixares. He never tired of the walk up the *Gomerez* and the quiet that the tree-lined *Paseo* offered. He always did his best thinking here, losing himself in another time. It was always then that he best connected with all that was Granada. Arriving at the hotel, the night clerk Alberto greeted him at reception as he passed through the lobby.

"*Señor ... tiene un mensaje*" (You have a message).

He wondered why Nadya might send him something when he was sure to see her the next day.

Reaching for the note from the clerk, Carlos thanked Alberto and walked over to the far side of the lobby to the service bar where Antonio was closing up.

"*Deseas algo Carlos?*" (Would you care for something?)

Carlos sat on one of the high stools and ordered a café con leche and opened the envelope he was just handed. It was a short note of only two lines that read,

*Your presence is requested at the office of Inspector De Los Rios at the soonest convenient time at the central police station located at Plaza Campo 3. Thanking you in advance.*

The Secretary of Inspectors of the Granada Provincial Police had signed it. Carlos stared at the note in amazement. The first thought that entered his head was that they were on to Neftali. But what could he say or do about this. Antonio looked at Carlos and asked, "Is anything wrong, Señor?"

Carlos shook his head indicating that he was alright. Taking two big gulps of his coffee, he bid Antonio goodnight and approached the stairway to his room. He wondered if he should call Nadya or Neftali but reasoned that it would only cause alarm and decided against it. There was no need to frighten them and he could always talk to them later. How did the inspector even know of him? He must be watching.

Once in his room, Carlos opened the window to let what little breeze there was trickle in. It took several hours for him to fall asleep while he went over and over what he might say to the inspector. The night passed slowly and Carlos slept poorly, but was relieved when the first dawn appeared. He rose quickly to shower and shave and planned to go to the station first thing. The anticipation made his body stiff, but he hoped that he could act casually so that the inspector might not notice his fear.

Carlos made his way downtown, arriving at the station shortly past ten a.m. After stopping at the reception desk, an officer directed him to the right corner office at the top of the stairs. He found the office easily and knocked at the door. A man in his late sixties answered the door dressed in a light summer cotton suit with a white shirt opened at the neck. He looked at Carlos and smiled, "Come in. You must be my friend from the Albayzin—thank you so much for answering my request so quickly. Please come in and have a seat. May I offer you a beverage?"

Carlos shook his hand and told him that water would be fine. Finding his way to the only available chair in the room, Carlos sat down and took in the stark surroundings. He kept thinking to himself how nervous he must appear, but hoped the inspector would not pick up on the fact that he was trembling.

"What can I do for you sir? Have I done something wrong?"

The inspector's eyes remained fixed on his and Carlos felt that he was staring right through him. Then, he smiled again.

"Let me get right to the point sir ..." He did not seem menacing and Carlos waited for him to continue. "May I ask first what brings you to our city?"

"I am doing research in hopes of writing a book," Carlos replied cautiously."

Writing a book about our city? Granada has so much to offer, and what are you writing about?"

"Is there a better place to research the life of Federico García Lorca?" Carlos asked defiantly.

De Los Rios stood and viewed the young man before him for several moments, his eyes squinting. He didn't say anything, but his straight stare made Carlos uneasy. He had a look on his face that made Carlos feel transparent, as though he could read his every thought. That is why he is so good at his job, Carlos thought; it was a questioning stare as if to say, are you sure you are telling me the truth?

"Lorca, huh? You too? Lately, everything seems to be about Lorca in this town. The man is dead more than forty years and nobody can think of anything else but Lorca, Lorca, Lorca."

Carlos sat uncomfortably in his chair and answered quickly, "I suppose there remain many questions that have to be answered about the poet, and certainly all the newspaper accounts of the past several weeks have stirred much interest, sir."

"What kinds of questions do you mean?"

"There certainly is a lot of doubt as to exactly what happened in the last few days of Lorca's life, wouldn't you agree?"

"May I call you Carlos, young man?" he ventured, as Carlos nervously consented.

"Listen Carlos, the government has decided upon a course of action that many people in this city think is the wrong thing to do. I am sure you know what their plans consist of—they are in the newspapers every day, as you have just said. However, since this is the course of action that they have decided upon, we do our best to ensure that our citizens comply. Lately, there have been many rumors about the Lorca grave, have you ever visited the place?"

Carlos shook his head and the inspector nodded saying, "I thought you probably might have. That place is a stain on the people of Granada. Whether it was right or wrong, the death of Lorca I mean, it occurred a long time ago and people will not let it go. Many things happened at that time that should not have happened, but it is the past … Anyway, my office is involved in this because we think there is a plan to do something that involves this site. Of course we cannot allow it to happen. And you are here because I have a feeling that you might know something about this."

Carlos moved uneasily in his seat certain that the inspector had taken notice of his surprise.

He responded cautiously—"I go to the Albayzin because I am first a lover of *Flamenco* and second, I am seeing a young woman who dances in one of the caves."

"Yes, I know—the daughter of Neftali."

The inspector' reply caught him off guard and as he looked at him another smile broke across his face.

"She is quite a lovely young lady whom I have known for many years. You should not be surprised; it is my business to be aware of everything in my city."

"Aside from what I have told you, there is nothing I can help you with sir."

He looked at Carlos without saying a word and then spoke, "Well, thank you for coming in so quickly and I hope if anything that we have talked about comes to your attention that you will have the courtesy to inform me, Carlos."

The interview apparently over, the inspector shook his hand and headed toward the doorway. Opening the door, as Carlos was leaving, he added, "Please give my best to Nadya, Carlos."

Inspector De Los Rios sat down at his desk contented. He was now certain that between what he knew from Franci and the reaction of this nervous young man, something was afoot. Now came the easy part. All he had to do was sit and wait. As always, he was confident—a confidence that came when he envisioned the pieces of a puzzle coming together. And this puzzle was moving along just fine. He sat back, lit a cigarette and started to shuffle through the mound of papers on his desk.

# CHAPTER 29

R AMON RUIZ ALONSO stopped his car in front of the Rosales' house. It was August sixteenth — a full month after Federico had arrived in Granada. His face was contorted in a sardonic smile. He looked up the street while lighting a cigarette and saw the Police Assault Guards on rooftops and at every corner, placed there to ensure that the poet could not escape. He finally had discovered the whereabouts of this "son of a bitch" and he was the head of the operation to retrieve him and bring him back to the Civil Government's office on Duquesa Street. His plan fell into place quickly once the poet's location had been verified.

Ruiz Alonso had spent days going back and forth to the Lorca *Huerta* only to find the poet not at home. The family had been continually visited by groups of men taunting the Lorcas in an attempt to determine his whereabouts. On one occasion Don Federico, the poet's father, was struck as he objected to the intrusion at his home. The poisonous atmosphere in Granada affected even many of the wealthy families. However, Ruiz Alonso was insistent and returned often, continually on the lookout for the poet.

On his last visit to the family, Lorca's sister shouted out in desperation, "He is not here, he's gone to read poetry with a friend."

Ruiz Alonso knew immediately where he must have gone to take refuge. It had to be at the house of Luis Rosales, who was himself a poet and friend of the Lorca family. He was also a Falangist leader and Ruiz Alonso guessed that the family probably thought he would be safe with them.

His obsession was to apprehend the poet and personally take charge of detaining Lorca. However, he had to step carefully and use caution due to of the stature of Luis Rosales and his family in the Falangist hierarchy. The Spanish Falange had been founded in 1933 by José Antonio Primo de Rivera and was fervently anti-socialist and Marxist. They despised the reforms of the newly elected Republican government. As a staunch Catholic, Ruiz Alonso believed firmly in the Fascist state fashioned after the Italian model of Benito Mussolini.

Ramon Ruiz Alonso knew Granada well. He had been in Granada since 1933 working as a typographer for a magazine called *Ideal* published by the *Editorial Catolica*—a fervently right-wing periodical. Here he became a member of the Accion Popular, the conservative Catholic political party.

This newly formed, localized party was part of a larger, nationwide consortium of Catholic parties named C.E.D.A., or Conferacion de Derechas Autonomas, led by the flamboyant right-wing orator José Maria Gil-Robles. Ruiz Alonso was elected a deputy from Granada from this party that along with other conservative parties was part of the Republican government of the first republic. Later, he was implicated in an election fraud scandal in 1936 when the election results of Granada were nullified and the left assumed much greater power in the republic.

Ruiz Alonso had lost his position and the one thousand peseta salary that went with it. He knew Luis Rosales and asked him to intercede on his behalf with José Antonio, the Falangist leader. Rosales was not enthused by this request and refused to intercede. When José

Antonio refused to reinstate Ruiz Alonso and his petition to regain his income, Ruiz Alonso vowed he would have his revenge.

His stature now greatly diminished with the Falangists, whom he had renounced openly, Ruiz Alonso was left without a position or means of support. But his hatred of the left, with all its artists and queers, was intense. He would not let Lorca, that goddamned queer, off the hook—especially in Luis Rosales' home.

Despite these multiple setbacks, Ruiz Alonso remained loyal to the right and was well known as a henchman who could be called on for a variety of tasks. One of those assigned to him—which he sought with vigor—was the arrest of Lorca, whom he considered a Russian spy and degenerate. The sugar coating was that Lorca was here now at the home of Luis Rosales, who had done him wrong.

What authority Ruiz Alonso had and who exactly sent him on this mission has been unclear to this day. But it's beyond question that he detested homosexuals and Lorca's sexuality was widely discussed throughout the country. Federico was thought to be a homosexual even though such a topic was rarely discussed in conservative Spain.

Ruiz Alonso was crafty enough to put together a warrant for Lorca, which he had with him now. It was payback time for the Falange that had rejected him. Arresting the poet in the home of Falange leaders gave him a special satisfaction. When his knock at the front door of the Rosales home was answered by one of the sisters, Ruiz Alonso stated bluntly, "I have come with a warrant to take Señor Federico García Lorca to the Civil Government station for questioning. Would you please tell him I am here and that he needs to accompany me immediately?"

The sisters became frantic and called to their brothers at the Falangist headquarters but found that they were not there. Miguel, the youngest brother, was at home at the time and helped Federico gather a few things and prepare to leave with Ruiz Alonso. As Ruiz Alonso sat in the Rosales home drinking coffee, Federico, who had remained in his upstairs room, was advised that someone was there to accompany him to the Civil Government and he should hurry. Miguel promptly decided to accompany Federico to the station to ensure that he was treated properly and to guarantee his safety.

Lorca was confused and trembling. He thanked the sisters for their kindness and the three men exited into Ruiz Alonso's car for the short drive to the station. Federico immediately recognized this Ramon Ruiz Alonso as the same man he saw on the train from Madrid—from whom he tried to hide and who he called a lizard. He cried, "What possible reason could they have for arresting me? I am a friend of the Falange!"

In the few short minutes that it took them to arrive at the station, Federico appeared to have floated off into another dimension. He was fragile. He chain-smoked cigarettes and spoke nervously with Miguel, not understanding why he was being detained. He was confused and jabbered almost incoherently. He begged Ruiz Alonso to let him go as he kept repeating, what interest could they possibly have in him? He knew of the executions that were happening daily and of the plight of his brother-in-law. Those persistent thoughts of death that had always accompanied him were now clearly planted in his mind. Something deep inside Lorca had always suggested that his life could be compared to one of his tragic plays. He felt he was now living his own tragedy written by an unknown author.

Death had always been on his mind and now confronted him face-to-face. He thought of *Yerma* and *Bodas de Sangre*, his two plays that dealt with death and deceit and shivered at how his own play was now unfolding. His eyes were wide open and perspiration dripped from his forehead. His black hair hung down in his face.

Arriving at the station, he was directed upstairs to a private room. It was not customary for prisoners to be brought to this site. But, he was a special prisoner and would be treated differently. But then again, nothing in Lorca's short life was ever customary.

When Luis Rosales received notice of what had occurred, he went immediately to the station, completely enraged.

"Who here had the authority to enter my home, the home of a Falangist loyalist, and remove a guest of mine without consulting me?" he boomed.

Ruiz Alonso, smirking, stepped forward to say that he was the responsible one but was merely carrying out orders.

"You! You again?! Orders from whom, and by what authority? What is it that the poet has done?" barked Rosales.

"He has done more damage with his pen than he could with any bullet," sneered Ruiz Alonso, gloating at witnessing the discomfort of the same Rosales who had refused to help him maintain his rank.

"How dare you talk to me in that manner! Who are you to judge anything, you bastard?!" screamed Rosales. "Salute and don't show your face to me again."

The police officials hurried Ruiz Alonso out of the station and assured Rosales that there had been orders from higher-ups and that the whole case would be reviewed. Luis required the help of José Rosales, the eldest Rosales brother, who sought a meeting with Valdez Guzman, the newly appointed rebel commander of Granada. Guzman was surprised, for he apparently had not given the order to arrest the poet. He said that Lorca would have to be detained in prison for several days while Guzman investigated the charges. He assured José Rosales that a full review would occur. That review never was to be. Luis Rosales, still infuriated, came to the station and read a full indictment of Ruiz Alonso and the improper actions of Valdez Guzman.

Ruiz Alonso needed help against the powerful Rosales family. He went to speak with Valdez Guzman to convince him that the poet was a subversive, anti-Catholic, and a pervert. He was incensed that the Rosales family could protect such an enemy. But as it turned out, the Rosales' protest fell on deaf ears, as the rest of the story is history.

Lorca was removed and executed the very next morning while Valdez Guzman, angered at Luis Rosales for his actions, had him removed from the party and fined for his participation in accommodating Lorca.

# CHAPTER 30

SINCE CARLOS had decided to adapt these events to novel form, everything became a bit simpler, as he would now have license to portray events that reflected his own understanding. What exactly *did* occur? He could not be certain. With the revelations of the Gypsies and his bizarre meeting with Inspector De Los Rios, there was surely enough odd material to make his novel unique. He knew the plot was still playing out and that this story was sure to become even more intriguing. Carlos also realized he could not finish, as no ending was yet within his grasp. He began thinking about a possible title to the work, never settling on something that moved him.

Now his days were spent writing and proofing in the library. On some of those days, he just sat and stared at what he had written, disgusted. On other occasions, he was unable to pen even a whole paragraph. He sensed that everything could change in an instant if some new revelation became known. Carlos not only felt that this was bound to happen, but was inevitable.

During his constant trips to Viznar, he continually made attempts to contact people who had witnessed those days and who might add some further information about the poet. Mostly, however, he found people unwilling to discuss anything with him. The consensus of those who agreed to submit to interviews was that the poet was not even located there!—that the whole charade was merely a hoax for publicity, aimed at putting the Socialist government in a more favorable light. It was a bonafide political fiasco. Forty years of this farce was enough!

The summer dragged on slowly. Nothing new revealed itself to maybe give Carlos a boost in completing his work, and he felt stifled, like the hot summer air. He wished that something dramatic would happen. Carlos hoped for just one more spectacular revelation that would jumpstart his manuscript. He needed something to tie the ends together—something with which he could feel some sense of completion and closure.

One afternoon, as he was leaving the library, Carlos decided to call Nadya and see if she would come downtown and join him at a café on the *Gran Via*. They decided to meet at a small cafeteria they both knew and agreed to meet there within the hour. Walking down *Reyes Catolicos* heading for the *Gran Via,* he thought he would stop and buy a small gift for his Gypsy. This was *the* shopping center of Granada. Carlos surveyed the assortment of tourist shops that sold mostly souvenirs of the city, the fine jewelry stores, bookshops, and apparel and shoe stores that lined the thoroughfare. In particular, one small, Moroccan store with an assortment of colorful scarves caught his eye. Inside, he surveyed the collection of silk scarves and in an instant, one with bright red and yellow embroidery jumped out at him. It looked perfect for Nadya, who made any color more attractive. He knew that she could always wear this on the city's cold fall and winter nights, and what's more, she loved to wear loud colors that contrasted with her olive complexion. In truth, the cold of Granada's winters could be as brutal as its unbearable summer heat. Carlos was happy with his selection as he paid the clerk, who wrapped it for him.

Just as he exited, he caught a glimpse of someone he thought he recognized across the street. He looked more closely and although he was fifty meters away, he recognized the figure as someone he knew. It was the police inspector De Los Rios.

Carlos thought there was plenty of time before he was to meet Nadya. Why not cross the street and say hello to the inspector? As Carlos stepped into the street heading toward the inspector a second person emerged from a doorway close to where the inspector was standing. Carlos peered at the individual and then stopped dead in his tracks. He retreated toward the shop, trying not to be seen by either person. He then turned his eyes downward, afraid he might have been seen. His mind raced with confusion. He made certain his eyes had not deceived him and turned again to get a second glimpse. There was no doubt. The person he saw was Nadya's father, Neftali!

What could he be doing with the inspector? They appeared to know each other. And why did the inspector call him in to the station? Of course Neftali knew him. Carlos learned as much when De Los Rios talked with familiarity about Nadya. But why call him to the station if the inspector could just as well confront Neftali at any time? Did the inspector think that he, Carlos, would divulge to him all of this business about the Gypsies and about the poet Lorca? No matter how Carlos ran all the possibilities through his mind, none of it made any sense to him. The only information he could rely on was what he learned by talking with Nadya. Maybe she could shed some light herself. It was time for him to speak frankly and see if she had shared with him everything she knew. He also realized that he was not a Gypsy and it was not unreasonable to think that he might be out of the loop. Carlos knew quite well that it was not within Gypsies' nature to trust anyone outside of their own cultural realm.

Carlos shortly arrived at the café on the *Gran Via* and chose a table outside. The summer was coming to an end, but this day was still quite hot and there were sizable crowds of people moving in the streets in short sleeves on their way to midday meals. While waiting, he glanced at a copy of *Ideal*, the Granada daily. On the first inside page

he noticed a small headline at the bottom, WORK CONTINUES AT
VIZNAR SITE.

He read through the story quickly and saw that it offered no new
information other than that the team of people working there had lim-
ited their investigation to one specific area and that within the next
several days would begin the slow process of digging. This process very
much resembled that of archaeology. Above all else, it was tedious.
Workers drew quadrant diagrams of each location. Each quadrant was
then divided into still smaller quadrants and given a number. Finally,
each smaller quadrant was dug by hand to a depth of no more than ten
centimeters and the contents strained through a screen to reveal whatever remained. The recovered pieces would then be cataloged and entered into the site's daily diary.

*"Hola Carlos!"* spoke a voice from the street as he looked up to see a
smiling Nadya dressed in a sleeveless yellow dress and matching yellow
high heels. She looked stunning and was always dressed to perfection.
Carlos touched her forearm and kissed her on both cheeks. Nadya put
her arm around his waist and pulled him to her. She must have guessed
that something was bothering him and spoke quickly.

*"Carlos, que te pasa?"* (What's the matter?)

Carlos did not bother to answer, instead asking a question, "What
would you like, *chica?* Are you hungry? The roscas here are the best in
Granada."

He motioned to the waiter and ordered a large *rosca,* an Andalusian favorite consisting of circular sandwich bread filled with special
ingredients, and a hole in the middle, similar to the American bagel.
He ordered the house special with ham, cheese and tomato and two
mugs of beer. Nadya turned and without hesitating, as she always did,
asked, *"Dime amor,* tell me love, what is it?"

Carlos looked deeply at this beautiful woman, knowing that he
was venturing into an unknown subject, an area that he might not be
allowed to question. "I saw your father with detective De Los Rios several minutes ago on my way here to meet you. It appeared as if they

were quite good friends from the way they acted in the street. They didn't see me, as I ducked quickly into a store and watched them from across the street. Is something going on that you are not telling me? I know that the inspector knows you. I related to you our conversation of the police station, but is there something more than that?" Carlos looked at Nadya quizzically trying to read her expression.

"*Querido,* I know this policeman as I told you before, but why they would meet in the street today I have no idea. Are you sure that it was not by chance and they just crossed paths? Everyone knows everyone else in this city."

"I am not really sure of anything other than they spoke for a long while and embraced each other when they departed. They appeared to be good friends. Doesn't that seem strange to you after De Los Rios grilled me so much about your father at the station?"

Nadya did not answer. The waiter arrived with their order and both ate hungrily, seeming to change subjects for the moment.

"I almost forgot …" Carlos reached for the bag for the present he had just bought, "… a little something for you. I hope you like it."

She looked surprised and smiled the big smile that always disarmed Carlos. She instantly wrapped the soft silk scarf around her neck like only a Gypsy could do in the most inviting and sexy way. The colors clashed perfectly with her dark skin.

"You look good in anything," Carlos offered, admiring his pretty mate.

"It is beautiful and I love it!" She leaned over and kissed him again, wrapping her slender, delicate fingers around his. How lucky he felt that such a beautiful woman had fallen for him?"

When they had left the café and began walking on the *Gran Via* towards Reyes, proceeding upward toward the Albayzin, Nadya spoke again very quietly, "Something is going to happen quite soon, but I cannot tell you what."

Carlos guessed to himself that many questions that gnawed at him were about to be answered.

# CHAPTER 31

T HE SUMMER HAD ENDED and autumn was just commencing. The number of tourists visiting Granada had begun to decline. The fall colors in Granada were beginning to emerge and traces of snow could be seen on the peaks of the Sierra Nevadas, just east of the city. It was a wonderful time of year in Granada as the streets were far less crowded and people were glad for the reprieve from the oppressive summer swelter. The business in the *Flamenco* caves dropped off as well, with most open only during the weekends or by reservation from groups making special arrangements. Carlos spent less and less time at Neftali's cave and was glad, for it lent him more time to spend with Nadya, whose schedule was greatly reduced. Most days he would walk up the *Paseo* to visit her home. They'd take long walks around the Albayzin, go down to the *Plaza Nueva* for afternoon coffee and sweet cakes, or stay in Nadya's garden with its pleasant aromas of flowers, which Carlos enjoyed the most. They hardly went a day without seeing each other and Carlos was welcomed warmly in the house of Neftali. His wife always prepared a special repast with Carlos in mind, which the family would partake of in the garden.

This was paradise to Carlos, and on the many afternoons he visited, the family gathering was accompanied by Nadya's grandfather on the piano. Carlos marveled at how this man had committed so many of the great composers to memory—Liszt and Chopin regularly, but Carlos also recognized the music of Bach, Haydn, and Mozart. He would sit and play for hours at a time without tiring, and Carlos looked on in awe at how he was able to lend his playing such passion. Ironically, he never spoke to the couple on these days. When not at the piano, he spent much of the time in his room where Nadya said he enjoyed being alone—sitting by his window, sketching the landscape just outside and birds that crossed his vantage point. He would then join the family for meals and always had a ready smile—though in actuality, it was an empty smile. He hardly spoke unless spoken to and then answered with a single word or two without, according to Carlos' recollection, ever completing a sentence. Most times he did not answer at all. Carlos studied the old man often. He would watch him shuffle across the room and sit at the piano for long periods before beginning to play. Carlos guessed that he must have been at least eighty. Always dressing in a loose fitting jacket and string tie, there was an aura of dignity about the man that, in Carlos' mind, set him apart from many of the other older people he knew. Carlos loved to be in the grandfather's presence.

On many nights, the couple would return to the Alixares and make love—in Carlos' mind, each time being sweeter than the last as Nadya gave herself to Carlos without hesitation. Carlos spoke often with Nadya of finishing his book—together they talked of an appropriate name for it. The one problem was the *ending*. Carlos believed that he could not give it a title until he had determined how the book would end. As Lorca's life had ended so mysteriously and with such confusion, Carlos felt his project was undergoing the same difficulty. But one title that always managed to come to mind was *The Sons of Granada*—describing the last days of Lorca. But he and Nadya thought it sounded hollow and that it would not stir any real interest for a prospective reader.

Carlos took great license in adapting the players in his novel to the history he had researched. He imbued many of his characters with traits that they may or may not have possessed to inject greater appeal into his story. He did, however, sense that what he had written was good and the story line intriguing. The research he had compiled throughout the summer was, if anything, thorough. Carlos truly felt himself living the last days of the poet, and sometimes became so consumed by his project that he thought of nothing else—to the point where Nadya had to constantly remind him of her presence.

Carlos obsessively fretted that his book lacked something—a nagging sensation that what eluded him he was incapable of identifying, but which always hung in the air like a dense fog. This would be the one missing piece needed to give his work real value—something to ensure that the public would find excitement in it and also continue turning the pages. After all, holding one's interest was the key to any good book.

Other days, Carlos was deeply depressed that such a delicate, brilliant, and sensitive person like Lorca could have been disposed of so mercilessly and perfunctorily. He could not fathom the kind of cruelty these men carried within to destroy anything or anyone different from themselves. It was so profoundly wasteful that Lorca, a national treasure in Spain, was murdered at the very peak of his creativity. Nadya noticed immediately when he fell in one of these moods.

"*Ven Carlitos,* come Carlos, let's take a walk. The day is so beautiful."

On most occasions, this was enough to change his outlook. Carlos appreciated Nadya for looking inside him and seeing that he needed help to escape this gloomy haze.

One morning, breakfasting in the *Plaza Nueva* as always on coffee and toasted bread, he bought the *Ideal* as was his habit. The first headline that he saw was too hard to miss,

BONES FOUND AT LORCA GRAVE SITE

Investigators have uncovered bones at the suspected site where the famous
*Granadino* poet, Federico García Lorca was suspected to have been
executed. The site between Alfacar and Viznar has been for many years
a source of contention between those who prefer to let the past lie and
those who want a final reconciliation. The team of investigators will now
take their findings to their laboratory in Madrid, which should confirm in
the next few weeks if they are actually the bones of the famous poet. Does
Granada finally have the answers it has sought for so long?

"Is this what I was waiting for?!" Carlos shouted out loud. Several
people seated near him looked over at his table surprised—noticing
there was no other person seated with him. Carlos was lost in thought.
Neftali's plan to steal the bones had not worked. There must have been
too many guards. Maybe they were the bones of the other three men
supposedly executed at the same site with Lorca—the schoolteacher
and the two *bandilleras?* There were many questions that flew in and
out of his head and none of them had any good answers. This afternoon he would be at Neftali's home and maybe this would present an
opportunity to bring up the subject again. The image of Inspector De
Los Rios embracing Neftali that day on the *Reyes Catolicos* had led him
to genuinely believe that there was something missing in this story.

Carlos could hardly separate the story evolving around him in real
life from the storyline of his novel. He knew instinctively that they
were thoroughly intertwined and inseparable.

# CHAPTER 32

SEVERAL NIGHTS BEFORE, two automobiles followed each
other up the winding hills leaving the city of Granada, heading
toward the northeast. An older Simca followed the first car, an
old blue Seat. It was the last Sunday of September and a special day.
It was the holy fiesta of La Virgen de la Angustia, the most holy of all
Saints' days in Granada—La Virgen being the patron saint of the city.
It was a day of celebrations—a special day when, for instance, people
choose to baptize their children, as well as one where young *novios*
make their first wedding vows. The festivities typically would begin
on the Friday evening before the holy Sunday and end with the *Proce-
siones*. The Catholic Processions are most notable during Easter week,
when the faithful carry images of the Virgin on platforms throughout
the city's streets. The procession is as old as the Christian faith and a
solemn rite of the faithful to outwardly display their fervor for their
religion, patron saints and Jesus Christ. As such, this procession is the
most anticipated day of the year in the capital city.

The night was dark and two cars moved slowly ahead in single
file. About one-half kilometer from their destination, they stopped
and extinguished their headlights. Their occupants emerged from the

vehicles and formed a circle by the side of the road. Neftali's voice was barely audible as he gave final instructions to the group of men. Some lit cigarettes as they continued talking in the brisk night air. A few short minutes later, they returned to their respective autos, but for Neftali, who instead proceeded to walk up the winding road. After a minute or two, he disappeared around the first curve, as the two cars remained parked—awaiting a designated signal. Fifteen minutes later, the first car started its engine and drove ahead with the second auto doing likewise a few seconds later.

As they arrived near Alfacar, the site of the executions, the second car suddenly sped up and tried to pass the first, which the narrow road would not permit. It then intentionally made contact with the rear bumper of the Seat. Shortly thereafter, the first car slowed down as the second moved in to bump it yet again. Both vehicles then stopped and the men jumped out—two with bottles of whisky in their hands, yelling frantically at each other. The autos came to rest exactly in front of the green security fences put up by the team from Madrid to prevent entry into the site. The resulting commotion was underway and the loud noise from the ruckus broke through the silence of the night air. One of the Gypsies from the first car took a swing at one of the occupants from the second. He was screaming indecencies about the other man's mother, his family, and anything else that occurred to him. Just then, two more joined by wrestling each other to the ground, and a free-for-all was in the making.

The chief of the security guards at the site could not help but hear everything that was happening out front. He knew well of Granada's festivities, but did not think they would have spilled over all the way to this remote location. It was the chief's responsibility to deal with anything that occurred at the site and he was used to dealing with tourists who wanted to get a closer look, but not with a group of drunks brawling in the street. He wished the local *Guardia Civil*—Civil Guard—was closer than the several kilometers distance their station in Viznar and the site. They could be called, but the delay in their arrival would not deal with the situation as it stood at the moment. The chief knew that his detail might have trouble dealing with these Gypsies, who sounded as if they were quite drunk. He knew the Gypsies were known for their ferocity, so he called together the entire complement of security—eight in total. They all advanced from their positions with night sticks in hand, following their commander outside the fenced-in area and shouting orders at the brawlers, in an effort to gain the upper hand. The street was now a sea of confusion, with the guards attempting to separate the Gypsies from each other.

Silently, as this brouhaha unfolded, a sole figure entered the site from the rear—slipping under the protective barrier and moving toward the plots where the excavations were underway. He stopped at the first perforation, glanced in with his small flashlight, and decided to continue toward the next, where he stopped and examined it in similar fashion to the first.

At this point, he stopped and surveyed the area around him in the cool night air while listening to the cacophony erupting nearby. With a small canvas bag at his side, he climbed into the hole. After a short time—perhaps a few minutes or more—he emerged, and carefully studied the grave site, being careful to make sure it appeared undisturbed. He also noted all the segmented markings of the quadrants used by the investigators and was careful to leave them untouched. As quietly and unobtrusively as he had entered, he withdrew to the spot from which he had entered, slipping through the barrier and disappearing again into the pine woods that enveloped this infamous hill.

Meanwhile, the team of guards realized that most of the Gypsies were too drunk to hurt each other and were soon able to restore order after some light taps with their sticks. The Gypsy driver who had bumped the first car moved to survey the damage on the Seat and noted that only a slight scratch on the bumper had occurred. After several minutes of shouting and mediation by the chief of security, it was determined that if they wanted to carry this matter further, they should take their gripes back to Granada and deal with them there. Agreeing to this, the Gypsies all climbed back into their vehicles with the chief choosing the two he thought were the least drunk of the bunch to drive. They turned their autos back in the direction of the city for the return home.

Half a kilometer later, they stopped to pick up a lone figure walking slowly down the road with flashlight in hand. Climbing the *Paseo* to the Albayzin, the cars separated, heading off in different directions. The Seat soon came to a halt in front of a familiar house in Granada. Neftali climbed out from the blue auto and walked slowly toward his home. Not even the light of the old farol streetlights could not hide the smile that radiated from his face.

# CHAPTER 33

FEDERICO SAT ON A COT in the corner of the room. He
smoked cigarette after cigarette of the sweet light tobacco that he
imported, preferring it to the usual harsh black tobacco of Spain.
In another corner was a desk and chair where he did not sit. How many
days would they keep him here, he wondered. The taunting from the
personnel here in the Civil Government building was expected, but it
frightened him.

He pondered death now more than ever before. He visited places
in his memory that made him forget the circumstances facing him
now. He was like a little boy, humming old songs he knew to help sup-
press the imagery of this dreadful place. His mind flashed back and
forth and soon he was able to block out everything around him. The
images he evoked were a movie of his life. Each new scene was an instant in time, a memory that he captured for only several moments before it morphed into still another indelible recollection. It was like a
newsreel of his life passing in front of him — minus the narration. The
flashing, strobe light-like rapidity of the images tired him but he could
do nothing to stop them. This was not unusual for him. As a little boy,
a dead bird found in the yard had derailed him for a good while — un-

til he was coaxed back to reality by his mother, offering special sweets and loving caresses.

He thought of one of his closest friends, Ignacio Sanchez Mejia, a bullfighter who had made the fateful decision of fighting one bull too many and was gored to death. Federico had written a long poem dedicated to his dead friend, *"La Cogida y la Muerte,"* (The Goring and the Death). He thought of that terrible day when in the bullring the boy brought the white sheet—*el niño trajo la sabana blanca*—to cover the dead *torero*. He thought of people running to help with *La espuerta de cal ya prevenida,* or buckets of lime, to cover up the blood. He thought of the death, *y lo demas era muerte, solo muerte.* Repeated thoughts of death were consuming him.

Next came images of his family's maid, Angelina who had brought him food and drink and cigarettes. How sweet and frightened she was, and how he mustered enough courage, something not his *forte,* to comfort the old woman whom he had loved and who had loved him since he was a child.

He heard few sounds inside his cell. He was completely oblivious to the confusion and clamor that enveloped the government building.

When two men entered and ordered him to stand, his face wore a blank expression without any color. His clothes were disheveled, his long black hair lain askew across his forehead, and his unshaven face lent him a look of desperation. He put on his shoes without tying the laces and stood in place as each man grabbed an arm and thrust him down a flight of stairs. People turned to stare at the fate of Granada's most famous son, looking away quickly as if they knew what was happening was wrong.

Federico was guided into the back seat of a black car. Several men were standing about the vehicle, giving last minute orders to the chauffeur and his companion.

Federico was now drifting to a different place. He was a young boy once again. He was lining up his dolls—actors for his small puppet theater, entertaining his family in one of the many performances that had filled the days of his childhood.

The car pulled away and headed northeast along an unpaved road with many bumps and potholes. Federico felt nothing. Soon the car was by itself along this barren road, continuing slowly toward Alfacar and Viznar.

The drive was uneventful until when, almost at the sight of their destination, bright lights appeared in front of the car. The two men in the front seat looked at each other and realized that they were being requested to stop.

The driver spoke first to his companion, *"Esto que es?"* (What could this be?)

*"Ni idea"* (No idea) was the reply.

They stopped the automobile in the middle of the road and noticed several men—maybe four or five or more, it was difficult to tell for it was dark and no other light other than their headlights illuminated the road.

One of the men approached their car and a deep voice spoke out in the dark, "We will take him from here."

The puzzled driver asked him "Why? We were not told of this. Our orders were to ..."

"I know what your orders are," the man's voice interrupted, "and what right have you to question mine? Do you think I casually wait on untraveled roads for cars to pass by?"

The chauffeur looked at his companion and the words of this stranger suddenly began to make sense. He got out of the car still unable to make out exactly how many men were standing around. He then opened the rear door and took Federico from the auto. The poet now seemed lifeless, slumped over with his head down.

The stranger greeted the poet courteously, *"Buenas noches, Señor Lorca, tenga la bondad de acompañarnos,"* (Good evening, Mr. Lorca, if you would have the courtesy to accompany us.)

Federico said nothing. The chauffeur and his companion stared incredulously at the new escorts.

One of the strangers spoke first, "As you know, this is a very delicate operation and you are not to recount to anyone what has occurred here — do you understand?" Then, for emphasis, he repeated in a loud and commanding voice, *"Not to anyone, do you understand?* You will respond that your mission was carried out successfully, is that understood? Any other response could put your lives in danger."

The stranger moved closer to the two men his face almost touching theirs and slowly repeated once again, *"Is that understood?"*

Obviously unnerved, the chauffeur and his companion backed away and answered, "Yes, it is understood."

Without uttering a word, the two men returned to their black sedan, started the motor and ventured back down the bumpy road to the capital, leaving Federico to his dismal fate.

The men left standing in the dark watched as the car departed. Federico stood among the group wearing the same blank, expressionless face. He seemed to be looking beyond life, standing in a rumpled heap in the middle of the road. Two men approached him, each taking him by an arm, and escorted him to a waiting car. After the three men were seated, a few other men entered and sat next to Federico in the back seat, as if to prevent him from escaping. The car's engine turned over and it sped into the eerily soundless night.

# CHAPTER 34

Y ES, YES ... *I have heard ... there was a disturbance at the site
... What can you tell me? ... No, I do not want a report on my desk
in the morning ... A fight? ... Between who? ... Some revelers
from the fiesta of La Virgen?? ... That figures ... Your men handled it? ...
Good! ... Was anyone hurt? ... There were a few bumps and scrapes but
none to our men ... Good! ... I will file a complete report from here ...
yes ... go ahead ... Ok ... there is one more thing ... and what is that?
... The men were Gypsies? ... Alright, I will make sure that is part of the
report. ... Is there anything else? ... No, thank you and tell your men that
it was a job well done."*

Inspector De Los Rios sat behind his desk. He lit a cigarette and
let the smoke out slowly. He hoped this episode with Lorca would
finally come to an end. It had been a long time—more than forty
years—and he was tired of it. But he knew he had to see this through
and could even see an end in sight. He started to think back to when
he first started.

He was young, perhaps nineteen or twenty. He was a uniformed
policeman like every other. It was 1936 and Spain had just begun a revolt that would reverberate forever. He had no qualms with the rebels.

He was glad that there was someone strong enough to move against this insanity.

The excesses of this Republican government seemed enormous. Every day there were demonstrations in the street, churches were being burned, and the sacraments destroyed. Syndicates were in the streets, refusing to work. All that was sacred was being questioned. Where was the order? There needed to be a strong leader, someone who could handle disorder and return Spain to some kind of normalcy. Francisco Franco, the general from the Moroccan brigade, appeared to be just the man for that job. He was a no-nonsense, staunch Catholic who was sure to restore the peace. He had already seized control of Sevilla and Granada and was moving quickly to seize even more territory. He was disciplined and had a good part of the regular Spanish army siding with him — not all of it, but a good portion of the officer corps, which was essential for a victorious campaign.

De Los Rios remembered being assigned to a detail in the Civil Government, but it was not at all what he had expected. He was brash and thought he would have the chance to engage at some point. Republican forces had surrounded Granada and he ached at the chance of seeing action. But here in Granada, he was commanded to stay.

One evening late that summer, a special prisoner was brought in. De Los Rios had no idea of his identity other than he needed to be afforded special protection. The prisoner was escorted by two men in a dark sedan and they moved quickly to the second floor of the building. Shortly thereafter he learned that the prisoner was the famous García Lorca, the *Granadino* poet of international acclaim who was being held here under guard. At the time, it mattered little to him who he was — De Los Rios' superiors must have had good reason to detain him. In other words, he must be a *communist*.

Later on the same night the prisoner was brought in and once his shift was finished, De Los Rios returned to the home of his parents. With dinner nearly over, the telephone rang and his mother was quick to answer as the telephone was a new addition to their household and to Granada.

"*Si', si' Nando esta aqui.*" (Yes, yes, Nando is here), his mother shouted into the telephone. She turned to the dinner table—"It is for you, son."

Surprised, De Los Rios rose from his seat at the table, anxious to see why he was being called, as his mother whispered to him to take the telephone.

"*Tio* (Uncle), *How nice it is to hear from you. How are things in Madrid? ... Terrible? ... I am sorry to hear that ... You know we share different opinions of this insurrection, but I hope all is well with you. What can I do for you?*"

He listened intently as his uncle spoke into the telephone. For several minutes he listened without saying a word, a frown forming on his face. Standing straight without moving a muscle, he listened for a long while. His face remained sullen while his mother sat nearby, noticing the concern on her son's brow. She stopped what she was doing and kept a steady gaze on his conversation. After a long while, the policeman responded, sighing deeply, "*Okay uncle, this I will do for you but I am not in agreement. I think it is wrong ... I cannot see how this might have any value to you ... You certainly are aware of the position you are putting me in ... You will hear from me as soon as I am able to discern something. Yes ... I promise ... Yes ... I know it is important to you ... Tomorrow I will call you. Yes ... yes ... tomorrow ... Goodnight, uncle.*"

De Los Rios hung up the telephone and slowly returned to the table, a look of concern on his face. His mother, equally concerned, asked why his uncle Fernando was calling from Madrid.

"It is nothing mother. He was asking me about the situation here in Granada and I promised to report to him tomorrow about what the real status of the city is. He thinks the rebellion will be short lived."

The uncle was a Republican official serving in Madrid as the Minister of Education and the consequences of communicating with him at this point could be serious.

His mother served a desert of flan while De Los Rios sat and wondered what he was getting into. What could Uncle Fernando do from Granada?

Emerging from his daydream, De Los Rios let more smoke stream slowly out of his mouth. Now, many years later, this whole affair was resurfacing. He needed to do his best to manage the events that were rapidly moving every day. So far, everything was going according to plan. Hopefully, in a day or two, the remaining pieces would be in place and all questions would be answered. The investigation team at the site would wrap things up and the public's thirst satisfied when all final determinations were publicized—that the poet, Federico García Lorca, was executed at Viznar and his remains discovered.

# CHAPTER 35

CARLOS ARRIVED at Nadya's home around nine o'clock that evening. He had been invited to dinner, which always was served at about ten. The Spanish dined late and Carlos had adapted to the custom with zeal—finding it a much more suitable and preferable time to eat. He especially enjoyed the late after-dinner walks he took with Nadya. At this time of night, the streets were full of people similarly inclined. He also found that he ate much less during the day. Breakfast was simple, toast with olive oil and grated tomato and coffee. He did not eat lunch that the Spaniards ate at two o'clock and which for the vast majority was the heaviest meal of the day. Most working people dined in the evening with just a light supper—usually consisting of fruit and yogurt. Largely eschewing the midday meal, Carlos would arrive at the bars an hour before the crowds descended to have a glass or two of white wine, along with the traditional *tapas* that was always served gratuitously with a beverage.

This evening, Nadya greeted Carlos warmly at the door and guided him toward the garden behind the house where Neftali was sitting, reading a newspaper and drinking a glass of *vino del terreno*, the local wine that was enjoyed mostly by the older generation. It was much stronger than most bottled wines and distributed without label or intervention by the authorities. Any attempt to control its production or use would probably be futile.

Neftali looked up from his paper and smiling said, "*Bienvenido*, Carlos. How are you progressing with your writing?"

"I am doing quite well. I haven't settled on a title yet and the last few chapters have me a bit confused, but your daughter's help has been terrific. I suppose I need to send it to someone who will read and edit the manuscript and make suggestions for improvement. After that, if they think it suitable, we will look for a publisher—but it is too early to make that jump. I am happy that it is near completion. That in itself is an accomplishment for me."

"I am sure an appropriate title will occur to you before long, Carlos."

"That also depends on how I decide the ending will look. Lorca's last few days have me really confused. Despite my research and the few interviews I have been able to conduct, I find the evidence so contradictory that if I were a good detective I would have doubts about everything. Nothing seems to be as it should."

"Doubts about what?" Neftali asked, putting the newspaper to one side and concentrating on Carlos. Nadya, who was sitting beside Carlos, sensed that this was the conversation that Carlos was seeking.

Carlos hesitated before he asked: "May I speak frankly, señor?"

"Please do," Neftali countered.

Carlos then began to recite the facts as he knew them.

"When we met, my initial attraction had been your wonderful cave and the interest you took in me. We spoke of Lorca, of Granada, and you helped me to understand what the poet meant to you—to *all* the Gypsies. You were so generous to share your music with me where otherwise I'd have no opportunity to hear anything remotely similar. I was truly pleased that you invited me into your home."

Carlos spoke slowly as Nadya moved closer and placed his hand in hers.

"You have treated me as family, which I appreciate greatly. I am in love with your daughter as I am sure you know. You took me into your confidence when I confronted you about your plan to steal the poet's bones. I even understood your reasoning for doing so. I questioned you no more about that—content to do my investigations and uncover as much information as I was able.

"My presence was requested at Police Headquarters. There, the Chief Inspector of Granada questioned me about my involvement in anything to do with Lorca's grave. I assumed that someone had talked to him about the caper you were planning. He knew of you and congratulated me on my good taste in pursuing your daughter.

"Then, to my sheer surprise, I see the two of you speak and embrace on the *Avenida de Reyes Catolicos;* after that, I didn't know what to think. I can tell you in a straightforward way that Nadya, who always shared her concern with me—always for your safety—offered not one hint about what might or might not be happening. Now, the papers report that the bones of someone—probably Lorca, I believe—have been recovered at the Viznar site and are being transported to Madrid for certain identification. So I thought to myself, what happened to Neftali? You had been so intent on recovering those bones before anyone else! Your reasons for wanting to do so were so convincing that I did not doubt for a moment your sincerity. But in the end, you apparently were not able to fulfill your plan. So right now I do not know what to think. But, let me continue if you will."

"Please do Carlos, I find this all interesting—"

"I see your contentedness—as if the discovery of the bones does not bother you. And I can't understand why."

Neftali leaned forward in his seat and from a pouch began to roll tobacco into a cigarette. His face did not reveal any unpleasant emotion. He finished rolling the cigarette, lit it and inhaled deeply, letting out a long cloud of blue smoke. He began to talk quietly looking first at his daughter then to Carlos.

"I had no doubts that we would eventually have this conversation.

Unfortunately, I am unable to help you at this time. It is a long story in which I am sure you will find great interest. My daughter, also, knows nothing of this story. I promise you that very soon I will tell you both everything that you wish to know. There will be conditions though and you should both talk together whether it is possible for you to accept them. I assure you that if you do, you'll be privy to information that is not known by anyone in Granada except for a few of my closest friends, and yes, they are Gypsies.

"It is not something of novels; it is something that cannot be shared. I would ask you to think long and hard, for it is the most astounding story that you will hear. If you agree, Nadya will let me know and we will meet again. Please do not make a hasty decision that is sometimes a fault of youth."

From the parlor, the soft music of Chopin filled the night air. The sounds from the piano brought the conversation to an end as Neftali stood up and motioned the couple to follow him.

"Shall we have dinner?"

As they entered the dining room lit only by candlelight, Neftali, Carlos and Nadya took their seats at the table, which was set for three. Neftali poured a glass of wine for each and as they toasted to good health and luck. In the background, the slow and maudlin notes of a Chopin etude lilting from grandfather's piano made Carlos reflect on all the events of that day.

# CHAPTER 36

THE FOLLOWING WEEK, Carlos invited Nadya to accompany him on a vacation. They planned to travel west to Cordoba, where the famous *mezquita*, the most impressive religious structure built by the Moors atop the Visigoth Basilica of San Vincente in the eighth century. It became the centerpiece of the Moorish Caliphate of Cordoba until its re-conquest by the Christians in the thirteenth century. It was the second largest *mesquita*, or mosque, in the Islamic world second only to the mosquita in Mecca. The couple spent hours walking through the ochre and white-colored mezquita, marveling at its architecture, with hundreds of pillars and intricate designs.

Carlos lamented that the zealous Catholics had destroyed a great part of the original structure to create a huge chapel in the middle of the mezquita. It is often repeated that when Carlos V, the King of Spain who had acceded to renovations at the mezquita came and saw what had been done, he commented, "You have taken something unique and transformed it into something mundane." He was displeased that such grandeur had been violated by his command.

The young couple stayed in the *Juderia*, of Cordoba, located adjacent to the mezquita on the River Quadalquivir, and traversed by the most spectacular Roman bridge that Spain possesses. This, the old Jewish section, had streets so narrow that the couple had to duck into doorways as cars came by. They passed several days in the street of *Buen Pastor* at a small hotel called Albucasis, named after a famous Moorish surgeon. The small hotel's staff pointed them to various locations in the city worth visiting, where they noticed the elegance of the Cordoban women, its exotic cuisine, and the cosmopolitan nature that Granada did not share. Nadya laughed when Carlos told her that despite the famous beauty of their women, no one could match the beauty of his Gypsy queen.

The couple then traveled from Cordoba to Sevilla, the city that has the most religious Catholic processions during the entire *Semana Santa*, or Easter week, where the faithful descend upon the city for its religious ceremonies. They promised each other they would return to see those sights. They walked the river where the site of the great mezquita, now a church, was constructed in the twelfth century. This glorious temple called the Giralda is the sister temple of another located in the Moroccan city of Marrakech called the Kitubia. The crowds of people in this, the largest of Andalusian cities, made Carlos feel uncomfortable. The poor reputation of this city with its ubiquitous pickpockets left him always on guard.

Carlos and Nadya drank beer and ate *tapas* and walked the streets for hours—visiting a museum on one occasion and reading the tourist brochures describing all the city had to offer. They were glad to leave after a stay of only two days in favor of their next destination, the city of Jerez de la Frontera.

Jerez greeted them at the tourist center at the city's entrance with a glass of their famous sherry, which they also called Jerez. The brandies and sherries of Jerez are exported worldwide and the people take great pride that no better product exists. Carlos and Nadya were excited to be here for one of the *Feria de Caballos*—or horse fairs—that was taking place throughout the week. The tradition of breeding horses was centuries old here, and Jerez had provided the

Spanish knights with the finest steeds as they confronted their Moorish foes. Each day a difficult event brought more horses with colorful dressings performing disciplines that challenged the imagination. They sidestepped in rhythmic cadence, responding attentively to the commands of their riders. Carlos and Nadya ate at the vendors' stands that provided the equestrian enthusiasts with varieties of local dishes, always infused with the oils and vinegars of Jerez. During the day, the lovers visited the monasteries and churches of this old city, and at night, their lovemaking reached new levels as they learned to please and satisfy ever more passionately the desires that each possessed.

Nadya carried herself with such poise and Carlos took much joy in watching her walk. He also enjoyed the ease with which she interacted with people; always lending full attention to whomever she engaged in conversation. She never judged the value of a person, be they lottery vendors or the maid at the hotel. At this time, Carlos considered himself the luckiest of men. He was the one she chose to love, and Nadya devoted herself to him—always favoring him with her caresses. He loved when she took his hand and brought it to her lips—kissing it with passion and affection. Their time together felt like a fantasy to him.

They briefly stopped in Cadiz, one of the old cities of the western world important for its role in the Punic Wars, which resulted in the Roman conquest of the city—the eventual port of embarkation for the Spanish explorers of the New World—along with the peninsula on which it sat.

The couple walked barefoot on the white, sandy beaches of Cadiz and imagined how it must have looked when Columbus, Cortez, and Pizarro set off toward their conquests. It was their last stop before heading back through Malaga, en route to Granada.

Carlos had not thought of the book for some time and was glad to take a break from the novel and Federico Lorca. Sometimes he had been so consumed by it that he wondered if he was losing sight of everything else. Nadya assured him that it was alright to take some time off and he would later be able to resume with new enthusiasm.

The pair was mindful of their impending conversation with her father and the results of the investigations in Madrid. Both of these events would write the final chapter of *The Sons of Granada*.

# CHAPTER 37

T HE NIGHTS OF GRANADA had turned quite cold, warrant-
ing a jacket or jersey as the temperatures plummeted to near
freezing—though the afternoons continued to be warm and
pleasant. Fall was fully upon the region and the yellows and reds of
the mountains surrounding the capital city were in full splendor. Ski
season would begin soon and the cold air sweeping from the snowy
mountain peaks into the *vegas* of Granada every evening was appreciated by those who detested the oppressive heat of summer. Carlos too
welcomed the change. Although the Hotel Alixares provided heat in
their rooms, he slept often with the window open, allowing the cold
night air to flow in.

Tourism was still slow in the *Flamenco* caves, which allowed Carlos and Nadya a good deal of time together. They visited the city's sites,
such as the Gran Catedral and the historic *carmen*s, and attended lectures on a variety of subjects offered by both the University and the
clubs of Granada. They particularly liked the history series conducted
at the University, which traced the roots of the city, its architecture,
and its important personages from the earliest of times. It consisted
of five lectures, with the final presenter spending considerable time on

the causes of the Civil War. He was a young man and delivered his talk with passion, clearly siding with the losing Republicans. He spoke of Granada's role in the rebellion and how it was instrumental in the success of the Nationalist forces. The presenter looked pained when he talked of the mass executions of the left—the intelligencia—comprising Granada's brightest minds, shot each day by the firing squads at Granada's main cemetery. Carlos spoke of Lorca with the professor and he agreed that Spain suffered much shame for his murder, and that the details of his death were murky and incomplete. The professor was adamant that it must have been due to personal grudges, as the orders were carried out without sufficient thought.

Spain's prestige suffered greatly for this act and Franco spent an enormous amount of time inviting back all the artists who had chosen exile to his regime in an effort to try and bolster his ostracized country. Few came back while he lived, but many returned after his death.

Carlos and Nadya invited the young professor to join them for coffee and he was delighted to have the opportunity to explain to them an importance of Viznar they had not previously been aware of. The young man told them of the *trincheras*, the World War I type trenches used here. This was the "front," the demarcation line between the *rojos* and the *azules*. It was a long, grueling battle led by Captain Nestares, the same officer responsible for the uprising in the capital city. Yes, Lorca's gravesite was said to be here, but the scholar also reminded them of the many thousands of people escorted there to be executed. In addition, the many dead buried there were from both sides of the conflict at the front. The professor took great interest in the novel Carlos was undertaking and enthusiastically requested to be among the first to proofread the final version, to which Carlos agreed.

Granada was also known for its "olive tourism," and the couple visited the local olive groves, learning how Spain's foremost product was grown, cared for and collected. Carlos and Nadya visited the sites where the fruit was transported to be processed according to its quality and grade, and made into oil. These were some of Spain's great olive presses and although these systems had been modernized over time, the final product still retained the quality that made Spain's oil renowned throughout the world.

There were several varieties of olive trees in the region—some being of much higher quality and thus more desirable for their oil. Still other types of olives were prized for eating, such as the *manzanillas,* included on most *tapas* in Andalusia.

The final "elaboration" played a significant role in the oil's quality. Consequently, some oils could cost many times more than others processed in the same presses, as the olives often came from carefully selected trees a particular landowner reserved specifically for his private stock. Carlos and Nadya tasted the different samples the showrooms offered their visitors, hoping to sell individual containers or cases of their finished products. Carlos decided to purchase a variety of samples to bring back as presents for many of his friends and acquaintances in Granada.

Carlos' novel was nearly done. He and Nadya carefully read it from start to finish, and discussed possible improvements. Nadya was an able and thoughtful critic who took an unusual interest in what were among the more arcane aspects of the book; for instance, why could they not know for certain who exactly drove Lorca to his death and who were the assassins? It was difficult to understand why so much was known up to the point at which the poet was removed from the Rosales' house. After that, nothing at all was clear. Nadya also derived great interest from all the passages where Carlos described the poet Lorca, along with his personal fears and dislikes. She would often suggest reasons as to why Lorca might have made the decisions he did, even as they would lead inevitably to his death. She thought of the poet as a delicate creature—someone with special abilities connected with the soul of Granada by some unseen umbilical cord. Lorca had been someone with a sensibility for the world around him neither seen nor shared by his contemporaries. His writings contained his own macabre visions of Granada—as if he had been born bearing the weight of its sad history on his shoulders. Nadya seemed to understand that the solea´—the deeply sad Gypsy lamentations of the *Cante Jondo*, from which Lorca wrote his book of poetry—was intertwined in the poet's being.

There were few that understood him and those who did were similarly gifted, such as, the poet Juan Ramon Jimenez; the artists Luis Buñuel and Salvador Dali´; and the composer Manuel de Falla—who took Lorca to Seville to reconnect with this music that was so intuitively a part of himself and which finally led the creative duo to salvage and restore this native Andalusian sound.

Why and how Nadya connected with the poet on this level amazed Carlos and he continued to probe her mind for insights, hoping they would lead to some final revelation he could include in the book.

The couple spent long afternoons together in the garden of her home, reading to each other from books they enjoyed or from newspaper articles. Their days were often accompanied by the soft tones of her grandfather's piano, where the old man passed an ever-increasing amount of time. Carlos inquired of her why the elderly man was so reticent. Nadya replied that for as long as she could remember—her whole life, in fact—he had always been that way. Her father owed it to the Civil War. Many of the older generation who had lived and witnessed the horrors that befell Granada in that era now seemed distant. It was as if they had seen enough misery and had no capacity for bearing anything else. Carlos thought this an apt description of her grandfather; he had reached some invisible emotional limit that would not permit him to express himself any further. He chose simply to play his vast repertoire of enchanting études and sonatas and pass his afternoons drawing in solitude and gazing downward at the city and toward its magnificent Alhambra, towering above. On one occasion, he handed Carlos a drawing of a leafless tree with a single bird sitting at the end of a long branch. It was a pen and ink line drawing, beautiful in its simplicity. Carlos profusely thanked the old man and tucked the drawing in the seam of a book he was given by Neftali on the elaboration of olives in Granada. He loved the old man's method of drawing and searched his memory, thinking he had previously seen examples of a similar style. But Carlos quickly abandoned this stream of consciousness when Nadya announced she was ready for their afternoon stroll down the *Paseo* towards the *Plaza Nueva*. She grabbed Carlos' hand and escorted him out of the house.

# CHAPTER 38

C ARLOS NOW WANTED TO RETURN to the states with his manuscript. Although incomplete, he felt it was time to take it to his friend Ana, an elderly woman who had promised him she would give it a fair reading and the editing it was sure to require. He asked Nadya if she would accompany him to New York where they could spend Christmas. Carlos thought there was no greater place in the world than New York for reveling during the Christmas holidays. Fifth Avenue, with its famous storefronts elaborately decorated for the holidays, was a sight that had to be seen at least once in in a lifetime. Carlos wanted to share all this with Nadya, whose only trip outside Granada had been to Madrid when her father brought her there to see the sights of the great capital. Nadya was initially reluctant to accept his invitation and offered up the excuse of having obligations with her father's troupe in the *Flamenco* cave. Neftali, for his part, considered the invitation an opportunity not to be missed and assured his daughter that he could find a substitute for the Christmas holidays when the caves would be busy. She feared the thought of riding in an airplane, with so much time crossing the ocean, but Carlos made all of this seem like an everyday occurrence and finally coaxed Nadya into accepting.

Taking his beautiful lover to New York would be a dream come true for him. He imagined showing her Times Square, Chinatown, the museums. He laughed inside as he imagined her face on a ferry ride around the great city with all of its skyscrapers and perpetually hurried people jamming its streets.

She decided her outfits would not do for the great city, so she and her mother spent the next week looking for a wardrobe that was suitable for the visit to the great city. Carlos begged her not to buy too much, because once she ventured inside the great stores of New York—Saks Fifth Avenue, Lord & Taylor, or Bloomingdale's—she would certainly want to choose among their offerings. She laughed when he told her of the cosmetics department of Bloomingdale's and how women locked themselves up there for hours, trying on all kinds of fragrances and makeup offered by beautiful saleswomen.

Soon the time approached for their departure. They planned to take a train to Madrid and from there, a direct flight to New York.

Nadya couldn't contain her excitement as she greeted Carlos at the door of her house the night before their proposed departure. He wondered what this adventure would hold for him with this beautiful woman he loved at his side.

"*Carlos, ven es la hora,*" Nadya said.

Confused, Carlos glanced at his watch, "Am I late for something? I didn't know …"

"Papa wants to talk to us—you and me—alone; not even mama can be present."

Carlos had anticipated this conference with some apprehension. Not every day, especially here in Spain, could a young man escort a woman for an extended trip when they were not married. He knew Spain to be a conservative country, though somewhat more liberal since the dictator had died, but still true to the traditions between men and women. These were traditions to be maintained and observed. Carlos was ready to ask Neftali for this privilege and to assure him of his daughter's safety and certain return to Spain. They found Neftali seated in the garden as usual preparing to smoke a cigarette that he had just rolled. His eyes were gleaming and he received the couple smiling and talkative.

"First, this ..." he said, as he handed Carlos an envelope. "It is a little something for you two to enjoy in New York."

It was customary for the parents of a young woman to give money to a couple as they went on their honeymoon, and Carlos thanked him knowing he had not asked for the hand of Nadya. He felt embarrassed, which Neftali sensed. "I know that you two have much future, take care that you always respect each other ... nothing is of value as is respect..."

Carlos attempted to reply to Neftali but was interrupted by the old man, "... and there is something I suspect you have been waiting to hear from me and now is as good a time as any to tell you a short story that you may *not share* ... which we discussed previously."

Carlos looked over at Nadya, who was caught just as much by surprise as Carlos. Neftali lit his cigarette and began to talk slowly, reaching back in his memory.

"It was an August night, you know, that they decided to take the poet to Viznar. It was hot outside as always when I received a telephone call from a friend. You mentioned you saw me with that friend, much to your surprise. Yes, it was detective De Los Rios. Carlos sat straight up in his seat, unaware that the topic of Lorca would be brought up, and concentrated his total attention on the old Gypsy.

Neftali looked at his daughter, as he seemed to float back to another time.

"Many years ago when he first started in the force, the rebellion broke out. Not being political, Gypsies stayed apart from the bloodletting that happened in this city. We never considered the outcome to be of any importance to us for we were treated badly by most people here in the city. But, Lorca was different. His soul was Gypsy. Every Gypsy appreciated what he did at the Gran Concurso contest, when he brought the *Cante Jondo* to Granada. He validated us, gave us reason to be proud. Then, when he wrote the *Romancero Gitano*s, he put our souls on paper for all of Spain to see. It was extraordinary. He solely was responsible for saving us and for that we owed him.

"The telephone call I received was a favor from my friends. The detective's uncle was an important man in the Republican administration from Granada. He requested something from his nephew that could have cost him his life, for I can tell you without hesitation that the detective was fully on the side of the rebellion. But, he granted his uncle's request. Yes, Carlos, I knew when they were about to move Lorca to La Colonia near Viznar and that they intended to kill him. This we could not allow. So, a group of us waited on the road to Viznar and intercepted the vehicle. The two guards who accompanied him were completely taken by surprise, although they thought us part of the plan of execution. They handed him over to us without a word. We advised them that their lives were at stake if they revealed what happened on that back road and that their response should be simple ... yes, it was done."

Carlos sat wide eyed, looking at Neftali and not believing the account he just heard. Nadya sat staring at her father and she could sense the feeling of pride arising within her.

"But, the bones! They found bones at the site ..." Carlos' voice rose emphatically, unable to comprehend all that he already knew, along with this latest revelation.

"They were Lorca bones, Carlos."

"Lorca's bones?"

"Yes, but not the poet's," answered Neftali, expressionless. "Bones from a different Lorca we retrieved in Madrid."

Carlos sat dumbfounded and found himself mouthing the next question, "But where is Lorca?"

Neftali smiled—a smile that suggested to Carlos the answer would not be forthcoming.

"He is safe, but markedly changed. That night weighed on him with a burden he could not bear. He has spoken little since and seems to remember nothing. It cost him terribly. He became a different sort of person, not given to the brutality that was happening. He was easy to hide and has lived a simple life ever since that night. He does not write nor does he seek further friendships.

"And with the discovery of the bones, the debate about Lorca should come to an end?" Carlos asked.

"That is what we hope," answered the old Gypsy. "The inspector and I have lived with this for a long time and it is time to put the whole matter to rest. I trust this does no damage to your intended book. Nadya has explained to me that you have been quite indecisive about how to end your novel. These things I have told you I am sure would make a great story line and I personally don't think anyone would believe it if this was how you decided to conclude the book. I have no objection to this, but, as I have told you before, our conversation remains here."

With that, Neftali rose taking the couple by their hands. "I wish you both a great time in New York and with the book, and I look forward to many stories upon your return." The old Gypsy then stood up to bid them goodnight.

Carlos and Nadya turned to go. She kissed her father and Carlos embraced the old man with a newly-found affection and loyalty. They planned on departing the following day, with Neftali seeing them off at the old train station in Granada. That night, Carlos held Nadya in his arms and stared at the stars, knowing that it mattered not what would happen with his book. He had lived a summer of dreams that was coming to an end.

# CHAPTER 39

T HE FOLLOWING MORNING, the couple was on the train to
Madrid. They were ecstatic, and Nadya—beautiful as always,
dressed in a yellow dress with yellow high heels and a ribbon in
her hair—beaming at her mate. They chose a seat by a window and
Carlos started to tell her stories of America, while she listened to his
descriptions of New York, all the while tightly holding his hand. In
Granada she strutted with a confidence that her beauty afforded her.
It was not arrogance but rather her natural being—the elegance of a
dancer who was innately aware of the centuries of history that had cultivated her sensuality. She was a proud Gypsy; but away from home,
she was uncertain, though still very happy. She knew Carlos loved her
as she loved him and she felt safe.

They decided to go to the dining car and celebrate their departure
from Granada. They sat at a table for two and a white coated *camerero*
attended to them. They ordered an assortment of *tapas* and a half bottle of champagne as the countryside sailed by. Carlos reached down
and took from his bag several books that he had brought with him. He
found the book of olives that Neftali had lent him, and as he skipped
though the pages, he came across the drawing that grandfather had

given him. He showed it to Nadya, who smiled and took it from him, recognizing it as her grandfather's. She handed it back to Carlos, who turned it over and it was then they both noticed something written on the back they had not noticed before. It was a small paragraph that read:

*Noches tristes y el cuervo grita,*
Sad nights as the crow screams,
*todo no es muerte, muerte no lo es.*
everything is not death, it is not.
*Las estrellas lloran for los amantes dulces,*
The stars cry for the sweet lovers,
*Viveran; si viveran —*
they will live; yes, they will live —

Below, there was a simple signature. Carlos stared at Nadya and saw the tears rolling from her eyes. Was it possible? He looked again at the paper. It was unique signature, scrawled in black ink. Nadya was sobbing, her hand covering her face.

The waiter came over to ask if he could be of assistance. "Is there anything I can bring you señora?"

Carlos stared down at the picture again and at the signature he had seen hundreds of times. He looked again to be sure. It simply was signed *Federico.*

## Neftali's Epilogue

While we waited for *that* car to arrive on that *hot* August night — a night I will always remember — we knew we were doing the right thing. Not one of the Gypsies gave a second thought when I announced to them my plan. Those were desperate times and looking back I can say that we probably acted out of sheer desperation.

I knew that that the poet had been taken from the house on *Calle Angulo*. How did I know? Here in Granada the Gypsies know everything that is happening in the streets, and an acquaintance of mine, a Gypsy named Raimundo was telling everyone that the poet, García Lorca had been arrested! Our community was shocked. The Albayzin was preparing to defend itself against the new rebellion, and as you know many lives were lost here. The people here did not have the proper means to defend themselves and the slaughter that occurred here by the military forces was terrible. Most of us, Gypsies, stayed out of the fight. We were not political and whoever might be the victors in that ensuing chaos would treat us no differently. We were indifferent to this war.

We needed to act. We owed so much to the Gypsy poet who had rescued us from oblivion. We decided that we would go to the station on *Calle Duquesa,* where the poet was being held. We would go there late at night when the guards would be the fewest and free him. Lady luck never gave us that chance. On the same day our plan was to be carried out, a boyhood friend of mine came by the Albayzin looking for me. He took great risk in coming here. He was a policeman. All police were supporting the rebels and everyone in Granada knew who the police were.

He wanted to tell me something, something important. He was brought to me by Gypsies wary of his presence. I told them I could trust this man who wished to speak to me alone. He confided in me that this very night García Lorca would be taken to Viznar to be executed. He was warning me of this for he had known that the poet was someone very special to the Gypsies. He told me that there would be two men escorting him there and that they would not be accompanied by any other security.

The rest was easy. We took two automobiles and left in the early evening for Viznar, planning to intercept their auto. At two in the morning headlights appeared. Our men stepped into the roadway holding their hand up to stop that vehicle. We were all armed and would have fought right there if the need presented itself.

The two guards were surprised by our intervention. They knew nothing and told us their orders were to deliver the poet to the commander of the Colonia in Viznar. I threatened them, daring them to challenge our orders that were to be kept secret.

When we took the poet from the car he was empty. I mean, the poet, he had no expression on his face nor did he say anything to us. Something inside of him had gone wrong. His face was a blank. Whatever happened to him must have removed the fear and terror he was feeling. He was a shell—lifeless and without speech.

We took him to a Gypsy family in the mountains where he would be safe. They nursed him and cared for him. However, he never displayed after that night any appetite for life. His life had been hectic, and words of all things were his allies. They were also his enemy. Had he not been so brilliant, so willing to set down on paper his thoughts and views of this closed Spanish society that he loved, he might have had a better chance to live. The man we rescued that night was dead inside, willing to bear no more.

We loved him and adored him. Today, he passes his days with me. He sits on his terrace looking at the city. He looks up at the Alhambra that watches over him. He too, in turn, watches over it. He draws what he sees, the trees, the birds, and the clouds. He plays the piano, the songs that are the only things that reside in his memory. I think he is happy. When my daughter was born, he took a special affection for her and she for him. Nadya never needed to know of his secret. She spent long hours talking to her 'grandfather' and never complained when he spoke nothing back. In time she coaxed a few words of response from him. She was the only one that could bring a smile to his face.

Now my beautiful daughter is in love. This young man has the same feeling for Lorca as we do. He is not a Gypsy but he understands the poet perhaps even more than us. He talked to me of the poet's great deeds, of his love for Granada, of his poetry and his plays. He loves my Nadya completely, that is easy to see. They both know our secret now and I am glad to finally share this burden with someone else.

Her lover is a writer. When he writes his story of Lorca I wonder how it will end. It does not really matter, for life is stranger than fiction. And if he writes this ending that I have related to you here, the world will finally know. They will laugh and I will smile. Have the best of luck in New York, Carlos and Nadya. The poet gained much fame in New York, and I wish you the same.

## Carlos' Epilogue

Our train ride to Madrid was a happy one. It was also a quiet one. Nadya sat thinking, I guess, of her life. She probably was remembering her childhood with her grandfather. That is what she told me later. She could not believe that we had spent so much time together immersed in the study of the great poet and that all this time he had been such an important part of her life.

After the shock of our discovery had passed, I thought how strange this world is. It reveals its secrets in so many unusual ways. Why was I drawn to Granada? Did my interest in García Lorca bring me here or was I drawn here to take part in this play? How would I end my novel? No ending could match the events of the past few days. Neftali has asked me not to divulge this secret. I swear no one will ever know this secret that Neftali has decided to share with me. He also thought that if I wrote what actually happened to the poet it would be appropriate and probably no one would believe it. I hardly believe it. Before we left, Neftali embraced me and told me I was a true son of Granada. No compliment could have pleased me more. I was keeping company with Washington Irving, the essayist and short story writer who lived in the Alhambra, who cared deeply about Granada's history and its favorite sons. I felt akin to Boabdil, the last Moorish king of Granada who surrendered his kingdom without a fight. He is a son of Granada who forever will live in infamy.

Granada's most famous son, Federico García Lorca, has reshaped my life. He has shared with me his soul through his verse and his commitment to Granada's origins. He would not let Spain forget its great musical traditions, its *Cante Jondo* and *Flamenco*. He reminded Spain of its social condition and of its responsibility to its people. He reminded them when they did not care to hear what he was saying, yet he never ceased to write about the isolation and pain that are part of Andalucia. Now, he has given me his love and she is my constant companion — my Gypsy queen.

Nadya and I are off for an adventure to New York. I feel as if we are about to let the world know some small piece of history that was too soon forgotten. But we are sure to return here for my mind is spinning with new ideas, with new stories of events from other times that have also been forgotten. I should write next about Boabdil, the last king. I should also write about Cecelio, my great grandfather and how his nephew robbed him of his wife. There are many stories of Cuba that should be, but have not been told. Granada is now my home; I truly am now a son of Granada.

## Inspector De Los Rios' Epilogue

De Los Rios walked down the stairs from his office. Once on the
street, he paused to light a cigarette. Everything was clear in his mind
today. He had reviewed all the newspaper accounts of Viznar. Lorca's
bones had been found and identified. Once and for all, he could put to
rest the worry that hung over him for decades. He had always felt safe
while the site of Lorca's execution was off-limits to the public, while
the family of the poet steadfastly refused to allow his exhumation. That
had all changed with the new government. He remembered the telephone call from his uncle in Madrid, who would soon thereafter go
into exile in America. His uncle had begged him to notify his Gypsy
friend of the hour that the police intended to transport their prisoner.
He urged him to reveal the location where he would be taken. He had
done all that and had long wondered why he assisted in this deception.
Perhaps, he thought now, that despite the poet's criticisms of Spain he
did not understand why artists or poets needed to be executed. Perhaps
he did it because he felt allegiance to his family. But all that was behind
him now. His friend of many years, Neftali, had told him that he took
care of the matter. He recalled the telephone call from the commander
of the gravesite at Viznar and knew instantly that the Gypsy had a

hand in that disturbance. He could not guess why at the time until he saw the papers headline, Lorca's bones found at Viznar. This was the work of Neftali. He never asked the whereabouts of the poet. The less he knew the better. Why the poet had remained silent all these years was also a mystery to him. He knew the Gypsies would never reveal anything to do with that day.

He believed himself quite clever in seeking the aid of Franci, who found out what he already knew was unfolding. This would supply him with the cover he needed if something went awry—if Neftali's plan failed. He surmised that the poet could not be out of the country, for if he was he would have surely resurfaced. So he must be still in Spain if he was still alive. His police instincts assured him of that. He looked up so see the Sierra Nevadas covered with a layer of snow and felt a cool breeze across his face. He hoped that the young man Carlos and the Gypsy girl Nadya would have a wonderful vacation in New York and leave all this matter behind them. It was over … finally over.

ACKNOWLEDGMENTS

*Sons of Granada* was conceived in Granada, not far from where the Spanish poet and playwright, Federico Garcia Lorca was born. I live part time in Almuñecar, a small coastal city in Granada and so dedicate this work to all *Granadinos* who have felt the pain and grief of having lost so tragically one of their beloved countrymen.

Special thanks go to Sr. Daniel Muñoz Frontana in whose small ice cream parlor I passed countless hours talking to all about Lorca while seeing up close their sentiments about the tragic civil war. It was here that my novel took shape and went to paper.

To Rory and Mary Savoy Read, without whose enthusiasm, support and direction, *Sons* would never have been possible. Their constant support and appreciation for the writing never wavered.

And to Heather Barker who convinced me that the work was solid!

And to my editor Chris Hartman who has spent countless hours advising, proofing, and suggesting what I believe only enhanced my story.

Lastly, to my wife KC who must have tired of my single mindedness while writing *Sons*, when little else was in my thoughts.

Thank you.

## ABOUT THE TYPEFACE

The text of *Sons of Granada* was set in Filosofia, a font from the foundry of Emigre, co-founded in 1984 by graphic artists Zuzana Licko and Randy VanderLans. The Filosofia Regular family, designed in 1996, is intended for text applications. It is somewhat rugged with reduced contrast to withstand the reduction to text sizes.

"Filosofia is my interpretation of a Bodoni. It shows my personal preference for a geometric Bodoni, while incorporating such features as the slightly bulging round serif endings which often appeared in printed samples of Bodoni's work and reflect Bodoni's origins in letterpress technology." —ZUZANA LICKO